W9-DEL-201

… **Two sagas** from different galaxies converge to thwart the brutal onslaughts of three malicious rivals!
Two thrillingly interlaced epic stories that will keep you turning pages.
"I couldn't stop reading!"
Sting Chronicles is a must read!

Amazing characters, phenomenal settings and brilliant solutions
to fix Earth's climate and environmental blunders!

The **Zqorsa-chyem**, a malevolent alien race bent on total domination, destroys anything that keeps them from their quest of acquiring superior **Kyorma'kren** technology: All that is restraining their drive for total control of thousands of worlds in thousands of Galaxies.

Just in time … Earth's Geological Consortium was alerted to the existence of vanished Kyorma'kren knowledge entrusted to a sentient AI … **'Sting'** … that could save Earth from annihilation … but first their exploration team must prove their worthiness.

… Meanwhile on an alien world in a distant galaxy …

Without warning, **Vellyr** is near instantaneously transported off **Kholesteria** into a completely foreign part of Universe-H.

"I'm suspended in some unknown territory of Space with no idea where I am!"

Enclosed in a transparent 'bubble', seated in the gyroscopic chair of his experimental **HoloSpheric Imager**, Vellyr witnesses a totally foreign planet under relentless attack. While panicking the attacking vessels might turn hostilities on the 'Bubbles' position, the '**Away-Event**' spontaneously terminated.

"… I'm instantly back in my lab, still seated in my gyroscopic chair, it's as if I never left!

"What just happened … or did it?"

Sting Chronicles

Kyorma-Sol

Episode One

Published by:

Habitology University Publications
Division of: Habitology Institute Inc.

emails:

DavidHastingsTheAuthor@gmail.com
DJH.Habitology@gmail.com

Registrar.HabitologyUniversity@gmail.com

Sting Chronicles

Kyorma-Sol

Episode One

David J. Hastings PhD

Other Books by David J. Hastings

Reignite Your **ZEST**

WayBetter Your LIFE: BodySelf
WayBetter Your LIFE: MindSelf
WayBetter Your LIFE: Tactics

The Beautiful Golden Butterfly

Force-of-Habit: BodySelf
Force-of-Habit: MindSelf

Become a SUDOKU Master
Become a SUDOKU Master Workbook

Habitology University Publications:

Habitology Practitioner Course Book
Habitology Practitioner Questions Book
Habitology Masters (MHa) Fulfilment Manual
Habitology Doctorate (PhD) Research Guidebook

Other Resources:

YouTube Channel:

23 Keys to WayBetter your LIFE
and
www.HabitologyUniversity.com/blogs

Dedicated to my Son Brandon.

May he always passionately seek understanding
and share his wisdom!

The greatest gift bestowed to everyone is capability to
proactively choose what to **DO**!

Inaction will certainly result in nothing.

DOing something - although it may result in nothing
has the potential to create something.

DOing extreme however, not just guarantees creation of
something
but will most likely spawn incredible!

Prologue

$\mathbf{A}$lthough the astonishing content of Sting Chronicles could provoke skepticism, and thus nudge one toward deeming the following narrative a work of science fiction … "I assure you; it is not!"

Declaration

The Geological Consortium certifies these Chronicles authentic and accurate.

Ratifiable particulars of the remarkable events detailed herein were compiled from three sources: meticulously maintained mission logs, the diligently authenticated documentations of participant science teams and the corroborated testimonials of involved persons.

This first 'Sting Chronicle' is a full report on the astounding events, which resulted in "The-Find". Divulging The-Find's incredibly advanced knowledge gifts, which recalibrates far more than Mankinds understanding of our Cosmos, will clarify transformations facilitated by the implementation of The-Finds advancements.

Scientific scrutiny of just two of The-Finds disclosures gifted from its vast knowledge storehouse substantiate that is not only our 'Universe-Container', which I recently tagged Universe-H, shared with many other sentient entities but also 'transport' to any targeted position within its "Vastness" attainable - nearly instantaneously.

Why the Universe-**H** tag?

This Universe container is our **Home**. As well, **H**ydrogen and **H**elium comprise about 98 percent of its directly observable mass. **Note**: My last name, which also begins with an "**H**", I assure you is coincidental.

Additionally, not only have Kyorma'kren gifted Mankind the knowledge of "transport" but also communicated their fascinating coalescence of kismet and science, which culminated in achieving transport capability.

It will help to understand the life-form called Universe-**H** if one stops thinking it a thing and readjusts to understand that Universe-**H** is an entity, which retains information via quantum electromagnetic memory.

Kyorma'kren teach Universe-**H** is a sentient entity neither corporeal nor non-corporeal as one dichotomizes but a fully integrated blending into its Quantum Matrix of those and many other states of existence: not conceivable or observable by Human sensory systems or neurology or its resultant limited technologies.

Later will be disclosed the reason this manuscript is titled **"Sting Chronicles"**.

Anomaly

Approximately ten months prior to the release of this chronicle, I was chosen to accompany my friend/colleague, Jeraimy Crystale (a field seasoned scientist, mathematician and explorer) on a clandestine, highest-priority mission into the uncharted interior depths of central Antarctica. I was mega thrilled to be involved in a mysterious adventure with Jeraimy and his illustrious team.

Completely unanticipated however was that the detection of what were assumed common crystalline caverns would soon provide the means to save our planet from two extinction-level events: The malicious attack by one of three brutal alien races - the Zqorsa-chyem; and a massive gamma-ray burst propagated by a star 1000 times our Suns mass, which went super-nova millions of Earth years ago.

Neither did anyone expect the caverns nor their artifacts to enable both rapid inter-galactic travel and near instantaneous sojourns to almost any location within Universe-H.

Unanticipated as well was the hand-over of many fantastic knowledge gifts: Some targeted to correct environmental blunders that have disastrously compromised Earths very thin atmosphere; others to restore fragile ocean and fresh water systems.

Contributions detailed in this chronicle are many. For example, the means to not only control world climate and localized weather but also rebalance atmospheric CO_2 and Ozone plus facilitate repair of many other humanity created damages.

Shortly after my arrival at the Geological Consortium's main research facility, Jeraimy - team leader of Operation-Urgency two - explained, "Divad, you will be replacing Caylos Semansen who was lead counselor and support specialist. "Due to multiple right arm fractures incurred during return from our previous mission," Jeraimy continued without pause "Caylos is unable to join this mission".

"Dangerous mission" I acknowledged flatly … and then added "what happened to him?"

"You are not wrong that our missions can be dangerous," Jeraimy responded affably "but," he added whimsically "that's part of the fun - eh!" To answer your question though," Jeraimy continued "the accident occurred when Caylos plummeted into a jagged crevasse when the ice-bridge he was integrity testing gave way! You are safe though," Jeraimy quickly assured; and then added while loudly chuckling "mostly!"

I chuckled as well. "Luckily other serious injuries were averted," I remarked empathetically "which, if I'm correctly interpreting the mission report, attributes to a mandatory safety protocol that requires tethering of team members while on Antarctica's treacherous ice fields?"

"Yes, tethering definitely proved to be a lifesaving strategy," Jeraimy affirmed wholeheartedly "as very likely without it, everyone could have been killed!"

Continuing my briefing Jeraimy stated, "As you know the first Geological Consortium mission called Operation-Urgency was unsuccessful. If okay with you, I will explain why once underway. This second mission is tagged Operation-Urgency-2 or just OU-2. It will be tenanted by you, me and a team of six additional multidisciplinary experts."

Once OU-2 was well underway and had traversed the first ice field, I asked Jeraimy, "What were the urgencies that prompted the first mission?"

"Thanks for waiting a few hours to ask your questions," Jeraimy stated appreciatively. "The first mission," Jeraimy revealed "was incited by troubling reconnaissance data provided from our cutting-edge, newly deployed satellite swarm called 'DeeGe' which," Jeraimy clarified "is an acronym derived from its purpose: To digitally chart **D**eep **E**arth **Ge**ological formations."

"Its primary objective," Jeraimy continued "is to map deep Antarctic structures: Specifically those that would expose both rare-earth mineral deposits and subterranean fresh water accumulations. What compelled DeeGe's chief science gurus to rapidly outfit and deploy an exploration team," Jeraimy stated emphatically "was prompted by three troubling DeeGe findings."

"DeeGe's first data-bundle unveiled a previously unknown network of six subterranean cavern-like structures," elaborated Jeraimy "whose deep descending complex was located at or very near to the middle of the Antarctic continent's South Pole. Two aspects were particularly significant. First, these structures had remained undetected for who knows how long. Second, they were located in pristine prehistoric rocky terrain far below Antarctica's central ice sheet."

After a short pause Jeraimy resumed with heightened unease, "Substantially escalating concern was when multiple DeeGe deep-scan attempts of the structures were unsuccessful. Appreciably intensifying everyone's worry," Jeraimy highlighted with sweeping hand motions "was when data-bundle-2 confirmed that deep-scan impermeability was a consequence of the atomic formulation of its materials, which totally rebuffed classification."

"Data-bundle-3 however," Jeraimy relayed fretfully "is what pushed alarm to highest alert! It exposed that every 60 seconds the deepest cavern was cyclically pulsing a highly complex and heretofore unfamiliar 5 second frequency-signature burst. Even more unsettling," Jeraimy exclaimed "whatever its purpose, it is still transmitting!"

"These three perturbing data-bundles," Jeraimy stated decisively "were enough to provoke unanimous committee agreement that some radical faction must somehow be cloaking these caverns; likely to fulfill some insidious plan. Thus," Jeraimy continued "decided essential was that a Geological Consortium team be first to ascertain goings-on: Rather than some unknown quite possibly hostile self-serving group."

Once essential equipment and supplies were offloaded from several "Ice-Cat" tag-alongs and our first nights camp established, I asked Jeraimy while we were eating, "Why was the first expedition you commanded to the caverns deemed unsuccessful?"

"The short version," Jeraimy stated with a forced smile "is we were unable to gain access to even the first cavern. The longer version," offered Jeraimy "is that we did successfully arrive at the target site entry point, and as planned navigated downward to the outside of the shallowest of the first six caverns. As you will soon experience," Jeraimy added "we accomplished Stage-one of the 1650 foot (about half-kilometer) descent via a well naturally camouflaged ice tunnel that DeeGe had superbly both mapped and digitally rendered. Although slightly narrower than its average 3 meter height this ice-corridor part of the journey was challenging due to not only its coldness and 20 degree downward icy incline but also our heavy equipment load."

"Stage-two of the descent, also clearly rendered by DeeGe," Jeraimy continued "was via a linked 1900 foot (half-kilometer) volcanic lava tube with about a 30%

downward slant. Trouble ensued," Jeraimy emotionally stated "when we reached what was ascertained to be the outer wall of the first cavern. Try as we did, 'The-Wall' as we decided to name it, remained absolutely impenetrable!"

"After three days of painstaking attempts to breach it," Jeraimy disclosed in a disheartened tone "the very difficult decision to abort our mission was upheld by all."

"Not to be permanently foiled however," Jeraimy stated proudly "the team resolved to recalibrate our mission! Our updated plan tendered renewed hope regarding how we could punch through The-Walls outer layer. We would return to base camp and re-outfit our quest with diamond-tipped drilling equipment, and then revisit the cavern … thus, this second mission."

The Wall

Although my challenging trek to the Antarctic target site spawned many outstanding adventures, I have for now archived my telling of all but one of my experiences, which I call "The-Find".

A three day trek delivered Urgency-Team-2 to the implacably resistant first cavern wall. As the team began the process of setting up camp, unpacking monitoring equipment and various drilling and cutting tools, Jeraimy asked, "Divad, do you want to take a look at The-Wall we are challenged to find a way through?"

"Absolutely," I responded enthusiastically "… can't turn down such an extraordinary proposition as that!"

When we were about 40 strides from the section of the area chosen for base camp, I noticed the rocky tunnel doglegged right at about 45 degrees. I was mesmerized as I closed the 30 stride distance to the shimmering red of The-Wall: It was spectacular!

"What do you think," Jeraimy said smiling "my private tour worthwhile so far?"

Almost breathless from amazement I responded "I'll say! Even with all Urgency-Team-2's narratives, my mental picture did not come close to The-Walls incredible awesomeness! Hard to believe from its look," I supplemented with a quizzical timbre "that this magnificent shimmering crystalline edifice is so resistive to one gaining entry."

"Totally captivating," I repeated to Jeraimy several times as I closed the five step distance to The-Walls shimmering façade. When about 3 steps away, "More than captivated," I stated loudly to Jeraimy "because I'm suddenly feeling an overwhelming urge to touch it!"

While Jeraimy re-explored The-Walls surface, I too cautiously reached-out and touched a shoulder-high spot: My hand tingled. Within a fraction of a second a portion of the formerly impenetrable wall - about the size of an arched double house door - just vanished; as if it had never existed. Startled, Jeraimy and I nearly tripped over each other as we turned and scurried several long strides away. Unbelievably, when we looked back toward The-Wall, now about 10 feet (3 metres) away, it was once again solid.

"Did that really happen?" Jeraimy and I blurted virtually simultaneously. For what must have been several motionless minutes we gazed at one another with a turbulent mix of surprise, disbelief and confusion.

Being first to regain partial composure Jeraimy said, "I think we should touch The-Wall again."

My response was rapid and squeaky. "No chance … contact is definitely your entitlement. Besides, I can still feel my hand tingling … well at least the memory of it tingling."

After a short ponder Jeraimy offered-up a convincing argument. "I'm feeling we should try again because no devastating harm happened to us on direct contact."

Although I immediately believed his proposal was more to do with delusion than science, I didn't convey this to my friend. "Hopefully your conclusion is accurate," I retorted with a slightly nervous chuckle. However, my adamant self-chatter was badgering, "You're not thinking clearly Divad … You're not thinking clearly Divad!"

Nonetheless, in a skeptical attempt to convince myself of the legitimacy of Jeraimy's conclusion, I vocally added my own (likely much skewed) self-talk rationales: "Yes … true … I was unharmed and, the tingling sensation I briefly experienced did prove innocuous."

Thus, after a slight pause to rethink my assessment (perhaps more to ponder my getaway options or foolishness) I said, "Ok … here goes," at which point we gingerly approached and both touched The-Wall at approximately the same spot as before.

BAM! The opening again immediately appeared. This time however I stood my ground. More than slightly fearful my hand would be encased in crystal (or whatever The-Walls substance was) I very cautiously moved my hand into what I later christened "Opening-1". I was simultaneously amazed and grateful when my hand went through and was reclaimed intact … as if no barrier had existed.

No doubt because I was outright spellbound, I threw all caution to the wind and walked through the opening. I was beyond excited when I realized I was standing on the inside of the first cavern where no one had been before. I excitedly declared to Jeraimy "You should come through as well!"

Even though my invitation resulted in Jeraimy looking rather more than hesitant, his adventurer instincts quickly overpowered his cautious judgment and he boldly stepped through. "Fantastic," Jeraimy exclaimed in a grateful but loud trembling voice that echoed throughout the previously inaccessible cavern "What an amazing turn of events (events … events)!"

After perusing the splendor of the shimmering cavern all around us for what must have been ten minutes, I somewhat indecisively commented, "Jeraimy, I don't think we need our helmet lights: the inside perimeter of the entire cavern seems to be glowing."

After several additional seconds of visually scanning the inside walls, Jeraimy added his own very excited confirmation. "You are spot-on: The entire inside perimeter of the cavern is luminous … it's plenty bright!" At this, we both switched off our lights.

"Incredible," we blurted - once again almost simultaneously! Mesmerized unlike I have never experienced, I murmured, "Way, way and way beyond incredible!"

"I think prudent would be to scribe a first-impressions log. What do you think Jeraimy?" I posited.

"Great idea," he heartily confirmed! At that I dictated the following into my mobile device I call MOD.

"This first cavern, which slopes downward at about 10 degrees, is a cornerless elliptical tube whose crystalline-like perimeter glows a lustrous red. Laser measure verifies it as 30 meters (about 100 feet) long, 10 meters (about 30 feet) high, with majestically curved 'sides' 15 meters (about 50 feet) apart."

"At the far end of this first cavern, which for clarity I tag 'C-one', another shimmering wall is visible. From Jeraimy's and my current vantage points, a few steps inside what we have named Opening-1, the second wall at the far end appears very similar to the one that just allowed our entry by vanishing."

"Anything you would like to add?" I asked Jeraimy.

"All good," Jeraimy responded approvingly.

After a short pro-and-con debate, Jeraimy and I decided we should cautiously walk toward the far wall. We both focused on stepping cautiously along the sloped, slightly rough crystalline floor. We were a few steps from what I gauged C-one's halfway point, when I noticed a slight change in luminescence. Reflexively, I looked back toward our starting point and then abruptly screeched in fear. "Jeraimy … Opening-1 is solid again!"

As seasoned an explorer as Jeraimy is, he freaked and literally started running back to the once opening. I must admit I panicked as well! I also ran back toward what was once open. I was about five steps behind Jeraimy who was pounding on the wall when I arrived a second or two later. Caught up in Jeraimy's panic I hit the wall with the outside of my clenched fist.

The solid wall vaporized so rapidly we both lost balance and stumbled through and out. Reeling in total surprise, we glanced at each other as we lay prone on the outside floor. Without any hesitation we simultaneously jumped up and quickly scrambled away into the access tunnel stopping only when we arrived a dozen steps from the opening. When we looked back, Opening-1 had sealed-up once again.

I'm not sure if I was being brave or stupid, but I immediately walked back to the shimmering wall and touched it in the same spot as previously. The opening again just "appeared". Jeraimy must have had the same idea as he was right beside me with his outstretched hand where The-Wall once was.

We went in and out of the cavern several times with no more difficulty than walking through an open door. "I suggest we return to the mid-spot in the cavern where I think The-Wall changed back to solid and see what happens," I voiced convincingly.

"OK, sounds like a plan," said Jeraimy enthusiastically, as he immediately headed into the cavern! A few quick steps and I caught up.

"If we walk partly backwards," I suggested pragmatically "we can keep an eye on Opening-1."

Jeraimy agreeably responded, "Done and done."

Due to C-one's slope, the slightly rough crystalline floor, and stepping carefully sideways, we made our way slowly toward what we assessed to be the middle of the cavern. Just before we arrived at the anticipated mid-point destination, Opening-1 transitioned into solid once again.

"Incredible," Jeraimy said "it's either open or closed with no visible transition. Our team is going to have lots of fun figuring that out."

At this point we had no idea why The-Wall transitioned for us. I flippantly responded, "Fun if the transition occurs for other team members as well … otherwise not so much."

Jeraimy laughingly agreed and then questioningly added, "What do you think is the difference? Why did The-Wall remain impenetrable when the team was first here?"

"Wish I could answer those questions with confidence," I responded "but I have almost no idea why access has now been granted."

"I'm feeling a little safer," Jeraimy humorously commented "knowing we are not going to be trapped in this cavern until we horribly die." His remark was noticeably laced with residual uneasiness. "Shall we continue to what looks like the next wall then?" I posited.

Upon close approach I commented to Jeraimy, "This second wall looks like the first one, except for its color of course, which is more orange than red… right?" Without hesitation I was again compelled to reach-out and touch the surface of this second wall. This time when an opening appeared, I was even more shocked than the first time because Jeraimy was still a few steps away. Once again Jeraimy and I stared at each other in confusion.

Jeraimy stated matter-of-factly as he extended his arm through the opening, "The-Wall evaporated just like Opening-1."

Suddenly, Jeraimy went so still, rigid and pale, he could have been mistaken for a marble statue. Several dozen anxious seconds passed while I tried to rouse a response from him. Finally Jeraimy took a deep recovery breath and said in a trembling voice intermingled with wonder and disbelief, "Somehow, you are the key to opening these chambers!"

As I grappled the truth of Jeraimy bombshell, it was I who no doubt resembled a stone statue. After dozens of confusing rapid-fire thoughts, I sputtered in a high pitched voice, "How is my being a key as you called me, even possible: Especially after Urgency-Team-1 failed to gain access?"

"I truly don't have even the beginnings of a clue that would lead to an answer my friend," responded Jeraimy. "However, no doubt in my mind you and only you are for lack of a better word, 'recognized' by these two caverns or whatever they really are."

Struggling to reconcile the implications of Jeraimy's undeniable deduction, I asked in a tremored voice that must have betrayed my inner confusion, "So now what should we do, continue or go back for the others?"

After a short ponder Jeraimy replied, "Let's get the team involved and up to date with what just happened. Also, we don't have sufficient supplies or equipment anyway, so I definitely vote we get the others."

I was in full agreement with my team-lead friend. "They are going to have lots of questions," I mumbled without expectation of response.

"They indeed are my friend," said Jeraimy resolutely "they definitely are!"

As Jeraimy and I approached C-one's halfway point on our return to camp we both looked around at C-two just in time to glimpse its opening terminate. "Absolutely incredible," Jeraimy uttered "absolutely incredible!"

"Wow," I exclaimed with appreciation as we rounded the dogleg "the crew has been busy in our absence! I'm impressed base-camp set-up has been accomplished in such a short time!"

"They are an effective and efficient bunch," Jeraimy stated proudly.

"Hey you two," Skilyem the lead geologist said in a bright friendly voice "we were just talking about you guys …wondering if you had mysteriously vanished or something?"

"Definitely the 'or something' part," was Jeraimy's equally friendly, yet deeply textured response. "We have some crucial information to share, so please ask everyone to attend the operations tent ASAP."

Within minutes team members were assembled. Each sat on the ground near the operations chart, which graphically depicted a best-guess layout of the caverns and their surrounding terrain.

"What I am about to reveal," Jeraimy stated with emphasis "will quite possibly be the ultimate highlight of your careers! I'm told by Skilyem, some were wondering if Divad and I had disappeared … and … in a way we had."

"As Divad had not seen The-Wall," Jeraimy continued "I took him to see the barrier that so resolutely denied access on our previous mission. I'll get straight to the good-news surprise. When Divad touched The-Wall - as each of us has - a double-door sized opening simply appeared. Moreover," Jeraimy resumed over the resultant hum of surprised chatter "moreover," he repeated a little more loudly "the very same type opening happened at The-Wall of the second chamber as well. Seems clear," Jeraimy said - then after waiting several minutes for the team to quiet, reiterated "seems clear … Divad is some sort of 'cavern-key'. Extra good news though ... diamond drills won't be needed!"

Of course, everyone had copious questions, which Jeraimy and I answered thoroughly. Everyone was astonished and excited, but mostly me I think.

"So," Jeraimy stated decisively after all questions were satisfied "at the crack of what would be dawn if we weren't 1000 plus meters (about 3500 feet) underground, we will set-off in pursuit of answers. Please prepare survival items and equipment "for what I expect will be the most fantastic sojourn of our lifetimes!"

Cavern

My restless sleep was spiked with surreal images: I wondered if for others as well. While loading my backpack with crucial items scribed on my carry-list, distorted, disquieting images continued annexing my awareness.

Exiting my tent early, I was surprised to see a few others already downing hearty breakfasts. As I ambled toward the food table, I noted a small hill of backpacks and equipment partially obscuring the dogleg. "These folks are certainly prepared," I chuckled appreciatively to myself "I'm definitely in good hands!"

"Everyone's on the go early," I commented to Jasone who was carefully assessing the food table for a second portion.

"Yep," he responded in a friendly tone "seems like sleep was elusive to most last night. I for one am excited to see you perform your magic on that wall. Do you know I exhausted 3 days trying to crack it last time?"

"So I understand! Hopefully it will respond to my contact as it did yesterday," I said … then added with a smile "or we may yet be deploying the diamond cutters."

"Can't wait to find out," Jasone re-joined lightheartedly. "Let me put your backpack with the others, so you can get breakfast. Just trying to hurry you up," Jasone said with a broad smile that gave way to a hearty laugh.

"I promise I will eat quickly. I'm as excited as you are," I responded with a chuckle triggered by Jasone's forthright cheerfulness!

Just then Jeraimy's voice, which does not need augmenting with a bullhorn, rang out: "Please meet-up at the dogleg staging area in fifteen minutes. When all were assembled Jeraimy asked "Any enquiries before we head to The-Wall."

"Just one," Tristian, one of the geologists proclaimed "if the wall has revoked its rapport with Divad, do we get a refund?"

His trite comment was just what the group needed to break the tension: All guffawed heartily. "Humorous … but not funny," Jeraimy shot back with a big smile, and then said "let's head to The-Wall and hopefully through and beyond it." While looking and repeatedly pointing at me, he added with a broad grin, "No pressure Divad."

I and everyone laughed heartily in a way that highlighted the teams' anxious, expectant posture.

Standing at The-Wall, I surveyed each face: Evident was a mix of hopefulness and pessimism. Turning, I took the final two steps to the wall and touched it as I had yesterday. I'm pretty sure the whole group cheered simultaneously when Opening-1 appeared. The cacophony was comparable to the robust cheers of fans when their team scores the winning point in the last few seconds of a game.

"Quick warning and reminder," Jeraimy cautioned seriously "all must stay close together because yesterday Opening-1 sealed-up when Divad approached the middle of the cavern. I don't want anyone imbedded in stone," then Jeraimy humorously added "in this wall anyway."

Chuckles continued as all headed excitedly into the first cavern. Jeraimy entered last, making doubly sure team members and equipment were well clear of the opening. When satisfied, Jeraimy instructed, "All clear … Please move as a group toward the caverns middle as discussed."

When all were assembled near C-one's mid-point Jeraimy announced "As scheduled, the next 15 minutes will be utilized to gather any information about the composition of this incredible structure. If acceptable to everyone, this cavern is hereby designated C-one. Also," Jeraimy continued factually "all no doubt realize auxiliary light is unnecessary as C-one's entire perimeter amply luminesces."

Just as Jeraimy finished speaking, the once open doorway to C-one transitioned to solid. I noted I was standing about two steps from C-one's midpoint. Jeraimy came to me while the others assessed and explored. "Would you mind not touching the next wall until the whole group is ready to move on?"

"Definitely okay," I said "I will follow your direction and recommendations … you are Team-lead after all!"

"Thanks," Jeraimy responded then turned and advised the team it was time to regroup and share findings. When all had reassembled Jeraimy asked "Any shares?"

"Did anyone else notice the crystalline caverns red luminescence remains constant?" queried Scarlette who I later learned was a world class geophysicist. The crew nodded confirmations.

"Perhaps this 'red-light' chamber has another purpose," Jasone chuckled as he feigned removing his belt. Everyone laughed heartily at his insinuation! "Seriously though … one more observation valid this time, I promise," Jasone continued, "the entire caverns perimeter walls look uniform to me except at one spot, which is near the middle of the left wall at floor level."

Dyonne added, "Yes, I also observed only at this one location does C-one's consistent crystalline façade not only look different but also bulges conspicuously outward."

"Did anyone discover anything else like that?" Jasone questioned. Jasone and Scarlette who were Skilyem's Geologist teammates chimed in that they had both observed that the feature occurred only once.

"What is your take on its significance?" Jeraimy asked Skilyem.

"Although I and my two eminent associates," Skilyem the lead-geologist responded "have not had sufficient time to precisely evaluate all the geological marvels of this place, we agree this cavern is very old; very, very old in fact. Therefore, at this point anyway, we are gravitating toward concluding that 'The-Bulge' as we named it is likely the consequence of tectonic pressures being exerted over thousands of years."

"Thank you," Jeraimy acknowledged "we certainly have lots to learn. Anyone else like to share?" As all were silent, Jeraimy directed, "Well then, let's head to the second wall and see what happens ... remember, keep close!" With that reminder, everyone moved as a tight group to wall number two.

Walls 2 & 3

Once again Jeraimy ensured the team was closely gathered before he brightly asked, "OK who wants Divad to touch Wall-2?" As Jeraimy expected no dissenters he immediately indicated by nodding that I should take the final steps and touch Wall-2. When a section of Wall-2 vaporized as for Wall-1, I'm positive this ensuing cheer was even louder than the first.

I was careful to be nowhere near the center of C-two until all were through Opening-2, after which Jeraimy gave the heads-up to move as a group toward its center.

Once the teams 15 minute exploratory excursions were completed, several shared that C-two although similar in size to C-one is not identical. Although C-two's 10 degree slope was the same, both its crystals and luminescence were definitely orange, not red as with C-one.

"However," Scarlette reported "similar is that C-two presents an outcropping or bulge at the same relative coordinates as C-one's."

Although conjectures abounded regarding the purpose of the outcroppings differing features, no one was prepared to offer a solid theory. Nevertheless, discussions were unambiguous on one point: All were convinced clarifications would be presented as the mission continued.

Sensibly, the team decided to rename The-Bulges according to the cavern in which located. Thus, to ensure transparency, C-two's outcropping was labeled Bulge-2; whereas C-ones, Bulge-1.

"OK group," tendered Jeraimy "should we head off and see if C-three's cavern wall, which I suppose we will call Wall-3, is going to be as user-friendly as the last two and allow us entry? As anticipated," Jeraimy kidded with a broad mischievous smile "no protestors!"

"Remember to remain close together," Jeraimy reminded emphatically! Accordingly, everyone moved as a tight group to wall three. After double verifying the team was safely gathered Jeraimy quipped, "OK who wants Divad to touch Wall-3?" Imitating the crew's affirmations, Jeraimy indicated I should take the final steps and touch Wall-3.

When a section of Wall-3 vaporized as it had for Wall-1 and Wall-2, the group's quiet expectant stress immediately morphed to cheerful chatter. As all progressed through Opening-3, Jeraimy coached, "Two quick reminders: 15 minutes is allotted for exploration of C-three; the caverns center is our reassembly point. When after investigations all had reunited Jeraimy asked, "OK, who would like to share their C-three findings?"

Jasone was first to eagerly share, "According to my instruments, although C-three's length is twice C-two's, its width and height are the same!"

"Also," Scarlette quickly offered "C-three's glistening yellow crystalline perimeter also presents an outcropping that I'm assuming we will call Bulge-3. It is once again at the same relative coordinates as for both previous bulges."

"One additional observation the rest of my illustrious teammates have no doubt realized," Skilyem said in a flattering tone "is that cavern luminescence continues to present in rainbow or frequency spectrum order ... so far anyway."

"Thank you for sharing," said Jeraimy, and then added "any other discussion points?" When none were offered Jeraimy resumed speaking, "OK group, let's head-out and learn whether Wall-4 is as Divad friendly and permit-passage."

While approaching Wall-4, its difference was obvious! As I arrived within 5 steps of Wall-4, I shared my concern with Gustovan who was closest, "The vibrant shimmer displayed by the three previous walls is clearly absent ... right?"

"Yes ... you are not imagining that its surface is not only bland," Gustovan acknowledged "but even more strange is that the expected green color is absent!"

"Besides the issue with Wall-4's atypical appearance," I said to Jeraimy who was now also anxiously scrutinizing the wall "is that even though I have placed my hand over every spot on its surface, my touch doesn't produce an Opening: It just remains impenetrable, grey and unchanged."

As the crew intently watched my frustration grow with each thwarted touch, their escalating concerns were easily evidenced by the substantial volume increase of their anxious rumblings. After about 20 unsuccessful minutes, I turned toward Jeraimy. My face must have highlighted my extreme disappointment and upset because Jeraimy immediately proposed everyone take a 15 minute break.

Still standing at Wall-4 Jeraimy asked me, "Do you have any theories on why Wall-4 is - excuse the bad pun - stonewalling us?"

"I do not have the faintest clue," I said with a constricted squeak!

"Well," said Jeraimy optimistically "let's get the crew together and see if our exceptional brains can figure-it-out, OK? Excuse me everyone … let's take the next 60 minutes to set-up camp for the night. Once done," Jeraimy continued "grab some vittles and then gather together near Wall-4 so we can solution a positive outcome." Jeraimy added, "Oh … and bring any notes you think may spirit options or solutions."

Wall-4:

Options

Well before the allocated 60 minutes expired all had assembled and were chatting with excited optimism. Jeraimy took the lead, "As all would not only like to share their possibilities but also clearly hear other's ideas, I would like to give the floor to those who are ready to present well considered options. Additionally, I propose five minute uninterrupted presentation durations ... then ten minutes for questions and clarifications." Through unanimous nods, yes's and thumbs-up everyone agreed wholeheartedly.

"Okay," Jeraimy enquired "who would like to begin?" Almost simultaneously all hands went up! "Such exuberance," Jeraimy said with big smile "prompts me to suggest an addendum for establishing speaker order! How about allocating speakers reverse alphabetically by first name?"

"Well then, as everyone has agreed to my codicil," Jeraimy stated graciously "I believe Valerye, our resident Physicist and tech wonder has the floor for the next fifteen minutes."

As Operation-Urgency-2 team members were scientists, presentations and observations were clear, detailed and reasonable; as were responses to requested clarifications.

When each person had contributed - some several times, Jeraimy thanked everyone for their candor. "Obvious to me everyone is deeply engaged and committed to the success of this mission," Jeraimy said in a way that underlined his respect for each team member. "Feel free to update my distillation of the presented facts," Jeraimy continued "but of all observations, the one point that stands-out for me is how often The-Bulges were mentioned as a big unknown."

"Perceptive observation Jeraimy," Valerye remarked and then asked "Divad ... did you examine any of The-Bulges?"

"Actually, no I didn't," I answered, then continued by explaining "because I had already investigated the first two caverns with Jeraimy, we both remained near the middle while the rest of you were off exploring. Why do you ask?" I countered inquisitively.

"Here's my thought," Valerye responded "as you are 'The Key'," she emphasized "to activating the chambers Openings, I'm thinking maybe you are key to resolving the mystery of The-Bulges as well ... AND," she continued passionately "perhaps solving the role I'm presuming The-Bulges will play in your gaining access to C-four."

"Wow Valerye ... I think that yet another of your brilliant deductions," said Gustovan, the teams Medical

Doctor and celebrated Cosmologist. "Not meaning to be presumptuous," he said warmly "however, I would like to append Valerye's theory. "If there is a link," Gustovan continued "between The-Bulges and successfully opening C-four - and I think Valerye is 100% correct about that - then our cleverness is likely being tested: Probably, so none may enter C-four but those capable of solutioning a complex puzzle."

"In other words," I said with substantial levity "you believe we are being intelligence tested by the creators of this technology!" The group immediately burst into rolling chuckles and lively chatter.

About five minutes elapsed before Jeraimy interrupted during a brief conversational lull, "Seems both Valerye's theory, Gustovan's addendum and Divad's summary have great appeal to everyone. Divad and I are on board as well, so," Jeraimy stated crisply "let's devise next steps to either proof or debunk this working hypothesis."

"I would like to toss a compelling likelihood into the ring if I may," said Dyonne, the lead Physicist and technology wizard responsible for creating DeeGe's unique frequency scanning capabilities. All listened intently as she spoke. "I see events from a bit different perspective than most folks," she said matter-of-factly "because I deal in how understanding material vibrations or frequency characteristics enable insight into clarifying what things are and the way they work."

"When Valerye stated her theory," Dyonne shared "my thoughts linked three observances: First, luminescence; second, differing cavern colors; third, Divad's 'recognition' if you will by The-Walls. As all here are scientists," Dyonne continued "unnecessary to explain the frequency substrate of either luminescence or cavern colors. However, if frequency is either 'A' or 'THE' key - as I believe it is - then Divad's Vibrational-Frequency Signature must currently 'interface' with Wall-1's, Wall-2's and Wall-3's exacting security requirements, but as all have observed, not Wall-4's for some reason."

While looking around at his fellow team members Jasone stood up and asked, "Does anyone else other than me, not understand what Dyonne means by Vibrational-Frequency Signature?" All hands went up. "Dyonne … would you mind bringing us up to speed?" Jasone then added with a smile "a compressed version would be nice!" Chuckles again rolled through the group!

Dyonne with a big smile said, "OK my colleagues: I'll endeavor to keep my explanation as 'compressed' as possible without leaving out anything that might spirit an answer to our Wall-4 dilemma. I will require more than 5 minutes though: Any objections?" As no-one objected, Dyonne said in her wonderful lighthearted way, "Here we go then!"

Each person," Dyonne explained "emanates what I many years ago coined one's VibrationSignature. It is composed from two very different Harmonic-Signature sources I'll be explaining in a bit. As a preliminary note, I find amazing few realize they emit a VibrationSignature," Dyonne added passionately "let alone that theirs is absolutely 100% unique from any person who has ever or will ever live on this planet."

"I believe crucial," Dyonne continued "is for me to clarify why I'm sure Wall-4 is demanding a specifically augmented VibrationSignature. To accomplish substantiating my theory I will first detail functional building block concepts."

"First to appreciate," Dyonne emphasized "is that a person's VibrationSignature is a scientific fact; not hypothetical. Confirmable," Dyonne stressed "is that Mankind occupies a narrow frequency range on the Electromagnetic Frequency Spectrum (EFS). I am aware you all know the EFS provision's a linear scale upon which science relies to catalogue all energy varieties, elements, compounds, Life-Forms, species and even Universe-H itself."

"Both linear-frequency and harmonic-vibration of UniverseH's 'stuff' is not guesswork," Dyonne continued energetically "but science fact as well. Empirically, vibrational specificity is the fundamental Universe-H principal or Law that makes both existence and diversity possible. Clearly, without vibrational specificity," Dyonne elaborated "Universe-H would have mixed into a generic undefined mush many, many billions of years ago."

"I believe explaining the baseplate or BaseLevel facts of Universe-H, which are ipso facto the source of Divad's VibrationSignature," Dyonne clarified "will make clear why Divad is 'recognized' by this alien technology."

In order not to disrupt 'Sting Chronicles' storyline, Dyonne's extended explanations are available in the Appendix titled Dyonne-01.

"One VibrationSignature source manifests a harmonicFrequency, which is the consequence of the particular mixture and quantity of physical materials that comprise one's physical-self or Body (i.e., bio) mass. Applicably, this source is coined BIOVibe."

"In other words, as everyone is similarly assembled from uncountable BaseThree through BaseSeven ingredients, each person's physical-self harmonicallyVibrates or BIOVibes. However, due to BioMatter quantity variances between people, each person's BIOVibe is unique: even though perhaps variant only very slightly."

"The second source of one's VibrationSignature," Dyonne continued "which I abridged from ExperienceVibration, is EXVibe. EXVibe, which manifests as a holistic harmonicFrequency Signature, collectively represents one's storehoused experiences. It is uniquely propagated 24/7 from myriads of electricalEnergy frequencies or actionPotentials being constantly conserved and sensory-updated in trillions of cerebral neurons within both the Primitive and Cognitive brains, which forms the neural-storage real-estate I collectively term archivedOld."

"One can think of archivedOld as the sensory-collected forage whose retention enables recall and reconstitution into memories, imagination and inspiration. Know that whereas genetics dictates both BioMatter extents and brainMass capacity; experiences provide the fill, content or archivedOld that manifests one's EXVibe."

Conclusively thus, one's unique VibrationSignature is a harmonicFrequency holistically merged from both one's BIOVibe and one's EXVibe."

"Thus, as we have been 'allowed' to arrive at but not pass through Wall-4, my guess is that Divad's VibrationSignature requires the harmonization of another frequency or frequencies. Think of this frequency addition like a saxophone added to the harmonic created by a piano, guitar and drums," explained Dyonne. "Now I may be off my rocker," continued Dyonne energetically "but as Jeraimy pointed out, The-Bulges, which are the most 'unusual' cavern features, are also located very similarly. My hunch is they contain the means to augment Divad's VibrationSignature."

Reconfigure

"Thank you Dyonne," complimented Jeraimy "as always both informative and inspiring!"

"As a consequence of Dyonne's explanation of vibrational properties," exclaimed Scarlette "I'm theorizing that perhaps The-Bulge glow, which as we know is slightly different than their attendant cavern walls, is more pertinent than assumed. Perhaps their different luster is purposeful!"

"Cobbling together the intelligence-test theory," Scarlette continued "plus the differing cavern colors and the distinctive glows of The-Bulges in each cavern, could it be that frequency as Dyonne has so wonderfully underlined is key to their responding in some way?"

At that point Valerye, our tech wonder spoke up, "If we are being tested as we all agree we are and frequency is key ... I have a theory!"

Excited, Dyonne usurped Valerye's thought, "As C-one luminesces through the red spectrum and C-two through the Orange spectrum and C-three through the Yellow spectrum perhaps The-Bulges of each cavern are designed to only respond when the specific frequency and wavelength of their color is focused on them!"

"We should therefore," Valerye convincingly advocated as she resumed "reconfigure our Spectrum-Analyzer to also broadcast rather than only evaluate inbound frequencies. I am going to go way out on a limb," Valerye continued thoughtfully "and propose the first frequency burst should be the midline of red's frequency and wavelength, which I have calculated as 442 THz and 685 nm."

"Also, I suspect," Jasone offered his speculation "that The-Bulges will only ... and I'm going to use the word 'activate' ... when Divad is within proximity."

"I would like to add a caution to Jasone's theory," Dyonne injected! "To ensure no one becomes trapped due to Opening closures, I suggest the entire team with all equipment return to the C-one bulge in order to either corroborate or disprove our theory. Then if correct, all proceed to The-Bulge in C-two; then C-three as well."

"Anything clarification required or missed?" Jeraimy queried as he scanned for additional submissions. When none, Jeraimy said appreciatively, "Well ... this incredible team has certainly brainstormed a viable action plan. As no additional suggestions, let's get busy and make this happen by forming focus groups responsible to accomplish each task. For instance," said Jeraimy "I will assist our awesome Tech-Duo, Dyonne and Valerye, with repurposing the Spectrum-Analyzer to transmit frequencies."

"How much time," Jeraimy inquired of Dyonne and Valerye as the others listened intently "do you figure will be necessary to reconfigure the Spectrum-Analyzer?"

After a short huddle, Valerye responded, "We believe about three to five hours, however," she cautioned emphatically "that's only if we have the needed tools and can jury-rig the needed alignments."

"Alright," said Jeraimy "we'll get busy fulfilling that essential necessity while everyone else works on the other tasks, such as repacking equipment and so forth?"

Without any hesitation, the remaining six of us moved to the Operations tent where all quickly assumed responsibilities to ensure a seamless return to C-one.

During my packing duties, I would occasionally glance over to where Jeraimy and the Tech-Duo were working. Obvious they were totally engrossed in their critical task of reconfiguring the Spectrum-Analyzer.

I realized as no doubt did the others that the stress on them to succeed must be huge: because without the ability to transmit frequencies this mission would also fail. When my duties were accomplished and all group tasks completed, I headed over and asked Jeraimy if I could assist.

"Absolutely Divad," Jeraimy affirmed mischievously "the three of us definitely need our heads examined by your extreme Habitology and Psychology skills for thinking rejigging could be accomplished in three hours!" Looking toward Dyonne and Valerye, Jeraimy respectfully asked, "How many more hours do you require?"

"Definitely a few more," said Valerye with understandable apprehension in her voice "perhaps longer," she added as an afterthought.

"Divad, could you inform the others of our status and suggest they get some food and rest?" asked Dyonne respectfully "then, if you don't mind, grab us some food and water before you come back to assist?"

"More than happy to do anything that will support you three in your quest," I said jubilantly then added "feel free to ask for anything!"

About one hour later, which was near 8 p.m. in the world above the cavern, the conversion was completed. The accomplishment was marked by a three-way high-five and a few dance steps jovially performed by Dyonne and Valerye.

"Well done," I said cheerily "you three are miracle workers; no question!"

Jeraimy made the announcement after everyone gathered together in the Operations tent as I requested. "Hopefully," Jeraimy humbly confirmed "the reconfigurations that Dyonne and Valerye remarkably accomplished will 'unlock' … excuse the pun … the secret to Wall-4 access."

Very, very excited, everyone cheered! Over the next minutes each person individually congratulated Dyonne,

Valerye and Jeraimy for their incredible achievement. "Could everyone be ready to head back to C-one at 8 a.m.?" Dyonne asked.

Cavern
Revisits

"**O**bvious," I chuckled to Jeraimy when I met him on the way to the food table "from both the fact everyone is prepared at 6:30 and the excitement in the team's chatter, all are very eager to get to C-one to verify or debunk the bulge-theory's frequency/wavelength postulate."

"I'm sure," Jeraimy responded with a broad smile "we two are just as keen. Definitely great to see morale, confidence and excitement so high though," Jeraimy added "especially after yesterday's Wall-4 disappointment, which caused everyone frustration."

Breakfast done and final preparations completed I asked Jeraimy as we headed into C-two without issue, "What are your thoughts regarding Dyonne and Valerye's bulge-theory?" Before allowing Jeraimy to respond however, I offered up my view. I know my expectation contains no speck of doubt that Bulge-1 will respond to one of the frequency transmissions Dyonne and Valerye have so meticulously calculated … nonetheless, fingers and toes crossed, eh?"

Jeraimy laughed agreement and added, "Cross arms and legs and eyes as well!"

As we approached Bulge-1 the group, which had been noisily chattering, fell dead silent. Dyonne and Valerye were also quiet as they set-up and then verified the reconfigured Spectrum-Analyzer's calibrations. After about 10 minutes, which I swear felt like 3 hours, Dyonne said, "Our Bulge-1 trial run is good-to-go!"

"Just about ready," interjected Valerye confidently "I'm just performing one final mechanical adjustment to ensure the Spectrum-Analyzer's parabolic receiver is precisely aligned toward Bulge-1."

Once satisfied, Valerye gave Dyonne a go-ahead nod as she announced - so all could hear, "Here goes!" At that point, Dyonne pushed the momentary-switch for the 3 seconds they had assessed would effectively transmit the appropriate frequency and wavelength.

I was not the only one who was ecstatic to see Bulge-1 immediately glow a bright red and then open six flower-like petals from previously invisible seams.

"Something is inside," Skilyem said excitedly as he spontaneously reached to seize the object! Startled, when the 'petals' abruptly closed before he could retrieve the artifact, Skilyem turned and asked his teammates in a shaky voice, "Did you see that?"

"I think Jasone was right," Jeraimy recapped "when he anticipated that Divad would be needed to access The-Bulges. Let's try again," Jeraimy recommended "but this time let Divad attempt artifact retrieval!" Convinced Jasone was correct, everyone crowded around Bulge-1: hopeful to witness history.

As nods from everyone affirmed Jeraimy's suggestion Dyonne said, "OK … here goes," as she once again pushed the momentary-switch for 3 seconds. Fantastically, Bulge-1 opened once again.

Cautiously, I reached toward the now exposed nondescript small stone-like 'object' and without resistance removed it from its crib! The cheer was so exuberant I thought the crystalline cavern would never stop reverberating. Seconds after retrieval, as I held the stone-like 'object' in the palm of my left outstretched hand, its appearance dramatically transformed. Everyone hushed in silent amazement as the previously solid grey stone morphed to a barely visible translucent.

As the artifact was clearly of intense interest, everyone began seeking understanding by offering opinions. Jasone was first to offer an excited observation. "The 'object' is not totally clear but contains very, very thin 'threads', like spider silk, but of different colors … I count nine!"

As sharing our new discovery was fitting, I handed the artifact to Jasone as I said, "Better the artifact be in your hand while you examine it, than mine."

"Much appreciated," said Jasone "thank you!" To everyone's astonishment however, immediately after Jasone retrieved it from my hand, the artifact reverted to its bland stone-like appearance. "Wow," exclaimed an astonished Jasone as he handed the artifact back to me, "Divad really is the 'key' … for not only cavern access but also both artifact retrieval and transformation!"

"I believe you are correct Jasone," Skilyem said as he watched the artifact in my hand transmute into its transparent mode once again. "I would like to offer one more observation for which I have not even a faint explanation," Skilyem said as he scrutinized the artifact in my hand "whereas the smooth part of its surface is pitted with quite regularly placed shallow indentations, its jagged parts are not."

"Easy to grasp from the intensity of the crew's speculations," I brightly stated to Jeraimy "that they are thrilled about not only artifact attributes but also confirmation of Dyonne and Valerye's frequency/wavelength postulate."

Approximately ten minutes elapsed before Jeraimy interrupted the crew's spirited conversations to offer sincere congratulations: "Incredible deductions work everyone; absolutely incredible!"

Taking liberty, I said with a mischievous western accent and broad smile, "What dy'all desire: to start the trek home … or head to Bulge-2 and see what happens?" My ludicrous option caused snickers and loud guffaws to ripple throughout the team.

"I'm supposing," Jeraimy said with mock anticipation "the group's chuckles indicate everyone desires to head back to Bulge-2 and hopefully uncover more wonders!"

"Should I hang on to the Bulge-1 artifact?" I asked Jeraimy as the team prepared for its Bulge-2 revisit.

His immediate nod and smile clearly indicated he was thinking similarly. "As the artifact turns to stone for everyone else," Jeraimy said humorously "seems the only sensible option!"

"Just so you're aware," I stated while acknowledging his wit with a big smile "I'll put the artifact in my backpacks center compartment."

About fifteen minutes passed before everyone was gathered close to Bulge-2: All excitedly chattering about what may occur. Dyonne and Valerye were silent and focused as they began setting-up and calibrating the Spectrum-Analyzer to the midline settings for C-two's orange emanations.

In about 10 minutes, which I again swear felt way longer, Valerye said in her distinct spirited tone, "frequency 496 THz and wavelength of 605 nm have been entered and verified. We are ready for the Bulge-2 trial!" At this declaration Dyonne ensured the parabolic dish was suitably aimed toward Bulge-2 and - as she held the momentary-switch closed - counted out the calculated three mandatory seconds.

Everyone was ecstatic to see Bulge-2 not only emanate a bright orange glow but also open six flower-like petals from undetectable seams. "I can see something very much like Bulge-1's artifact inside Bulge-2," exclaimed Scarlette with huge excitement! It looks like a small ordinary stone as well! Let's see," proposed Scarlette "if the petals close-up when I reach for the 'object' as it did for Skilyem ... and then she added with her infectious broad smile "maybe it just didn't appreciate him like we do?" Everyone laughed heartily!

All watched in amazement as the "petals" immediately closed when Scarlette was close to retrieving the artifact. "Well, well ... that double underlines Divad's worth on this mission, doesn't it," Scarlette stated while looking at me with her signature smile.

"Seems irrefutable," confirmed Skilyem "Jasone was bang-on when he predicted Divad would be the key to unlocking The-Bulges."

As everyone crowded around Bulge-2 Jeraimy said, "OK, Divad, your second opportunity to make history has arrived! Again ... no pressure," he chuckled.

This time, like I was an old-hand at a familiar task, I boldly grasped the nondescript stone-like artifact, and as I had previously done at Bulge-1, removed it from Bulge-2's embrace without resistance! I swear, the cheer that rolled-up was much louder than at Bulge-1: I think because all knew we were back on track to mission success. As I held the artifact in the palm of my hand, its grey stone appearance transformed within a second to translucent: just as with the first artifact.

Jasone pointed out as before, "This artifact is not totally clear either! It also contains nine very, very thin 'threads' of different colors. Thorough examinations by everyone confirmed Jasone's count.

"Let's experiment," I suggested "and find out what happens when others handle this artifact." As everyone wanted to touch the artifact (likely to gain bragging rights when sharing this adventure story with family and friends), all were enthusiastically in favor. I handed the artifact to Jasone first. No one was particularly surprised when after Jasone gently plucked it from my hand the artifact reverted to its nondescript stone-like state.

Once the artifact had been passed around, Jasone exclaimed, "No matter what the combination, person-to-person or person-to-Divad-to-person the artifact only morphs to its transparent mode when solely in Divad's possession. Unquestionably, Divad is pivotal to this mission's success," he concluded with a mock bow that had all in stitches!"

"A quick re-mention," Skilyem offered when the chuckles had tapered "the smooth part of Bulge-2's artifact is also pitted with regularly placed shallow indentations. I hope clarification of their purpose is yet to come."

"Thanks Skilyem," Jeraimy stated as he addressed the group! I know our morning's quest has exceeded all my expectations. I'm sure everyone feels much the same and is anxious to continue. First though, as the time topside is a little after 1:00 pm," Jeraimy continued "I suggest we enjoy a 60 minute food and rest break prior to our trek to and encounter with Bulge-3. Better, to recharge ourselves now because I anticipate when Wall-4 'allows' passage no-one will want to stop pushing forward through remaining caverns."

After Jeraimy concluded, I asked him matter-of-factly, "I'm assuming I should hold on to this artifact as well?"

"Definitely," he responded with a nod and a smile.

"Shall do ... also though," I stated to ensure clarity "I will individually wrap the artifacts and store both in my backpacks center pouch. Additionally, in order to match their resident cavern number, I am marking their wrapping with 'A-one' and 'A-two'."

When the 60 allotted minutes had elapsed, Jeraimy asked in his friendly booming voice, "Everyone about ready to head over to Bulge-3 to discover if fortune still favors us cavern monkeys?" he amusingly quipped. Let me know when prepared," said Jeraimy "then we'll return to C-three and see what Bulge-3 has to offer."

Within minutes everyone was more than ready to continue our extraordinary adventure. "I believe this was the fastest I have ever seen a group of people assemble in one place. Are prizes for promptness being awarded?" I kidded loudly.

"Very humorous Divad," Jeraimy rejoined sporting a big smile "but as before with Jasone ... not funny!" Everyone laughed out loud!

When all arrived at Bulge-3, Dyonne and Valerye promptly went about setting-up and positioning the Spectrum-Analyzer (SA). "This time," Dyonne said in a voice loud enough to ensure everyone's inclusion "yellows frequency will be set to 517 THz and wavelength to 580 nm as these are its midline targets. We are confident they will trigger Bulge-3 to 'open'."

Valerye, comically imitating the humor of Divad and Jeraimy, crisply saluted Dyonne while intonating militarily, "SA is ready for deployment Mam!" Laughter was long and loud as none had ever seen Valerye so animated.

"Deploy away you two amazing experts," rejoined Jeraimy with a return salute that had everyone in stitches for several minutes. Utilizing SA's chronometer, Dyonne counted out three seconds while she held the momentary-switch closed: "One ...; two ...; three ...!"

Dyonne and Valerye stood motionless and speechless when Bulge-3's appearance did not change!

"Nothing happened! ... Oops," Jeraimy voiced in disbelief as he observed disappointment gathering on the teams faces. Probably only a few seconds elapsed (which seemed much longer to me) before both Dyonne and Valerye were back in motion.

"Okay, okay ... let's figure this out," said Dyonne talking loudly! "First, we know the red and orange 'bulges' responded to their midline frequency/wavelength combinations that Valerye calculated. Second," Dyonne continued while concurrently checking the Spectrum-Analyzer's positioning "we know SA is in the same relative position as for the two previous successes. I believe therefore," Dyonne said to Valerye in a voice sufficiently loud for the team to still hear "the problem must either be the frequency OR wavelength setting; OR the juxtaposition of frequency and wavelength! What do you think Valerye?"

As Valerye assessed the proposition, Dionne looked toward the others and asked, "Anyone have other suggestions?"

"I think I speak for everyone," Jeraimy said a few moments later in a calm tone that gave no hint of the anxiety he no doubt felt "and anyone correct me if I'm mistaken please, that we are confident with both of your impressive capabilities and assessments."

Valerye speaking so all could hear ratified Dyonne's hypothesis when she supportively stated, "Yes, I agree Dyonne because the midpoint of a frequency and its corresponding wavelength can easily be off by one point either way of midline. Know everyone," Valerye emphasized "that we planned for this possibility during Spectrum-Analyzer conversion. Therefore," Valerye continued excitedly "what we need to do is test each of the remaining eight possible frequency/wavelength combinations. I am sure one will work," Valerye added confidently!

In about 5 minutes Dyonne announced, "We are ready to apply each of the other possible frequency/wavelength combinations. Gather round folks, cross your fingers, and do anything else you believe brings luck!" Dyonne was standing at the Spectrum-Analyzer controls when, to ensure inclusion of everyone in the process, she asked, "OK Valerye, which combination are we evaluating next?"

Valerye called out, "Frequency 516; wavelength 579."

After verifying the agreed setting was registered correctly, Dyonne loudly declared, "Here goes trial two!" Then while pressing the momentary-switch, counted out the needed three seconds, "One …; two …; three …! No response," reported Dyonne "… what is the next combination please?"

"The next combination," voiced Valerye so everyone could hear "is frequency 516; wavelength 580."

After re-verifying the changed setting, Dyonne declared out loud, "Here goes test number three!" Then again she pressed the momentary-switch while counting out the three required seconds "One …; two …; three …!"

Everyone was colossally relieved to see Bulge-3 emanate a bright yellow glow and open six flower-like petals from its camouflaged seams. "OK Divad," a relieved Dyonne stated playfully "you're up again … good luck!"

"Happy to comply commander," I friskily responded as I marched mock-ceremoniously toward the now brightly glowing Bulge-3 outcropping. While reaching to retrieve Bulge-3's nondescript 'stone', the team was 'pin-drop' quiet as they eagerly looked-on with 'make-or-break' anticipation.

As twice before, I firmly grasped the peacefully nesting nondescript 'stone' artifact. I was thrilled … as no doubt was the entire team, when 'A-three' departed its Bulge-3 sanctuary without resistance! Within a second after my retrieval, A-three's grey appearance mimicked the transitions of the first two artifacts, and transformed to a clear translucent.

"Well," I said to Dyonne who was closest "from the resumption of joyful chatter, seems everyone is as relieved as am I!"

"I know I definitely am," retorted Scarlette who once again shared an observation. "This artifact is not totally clear either," she stated factually "plus," she continued emphatically "A-three, much like the first two artifacts, also contains nine very, very thin 'threads' of different colors."

"Thank you for sharing your observation," Jeraimy stated supportively. Noting the positive change in team mood from worried/pensive to happy/cheerful, Jeraimy stated lightheartedly, "Well, seems we've passed the first three tests," to which he accentuated a congratulatory compliment "well done again everyone … exceptionally well done!"

"As with the other artifacts," I confirmed when Jeraimy had finished conversing with the teams three Geologists "I will wrap A-three and put it in my backpack with the others."

"Thanks for not only keeping the artifacts safe but also ensuring I know where they are," said Jeraimy genuinely thankful. "Much appreciated!"

"From the look of everyone restlessly pawing the ground like corralled stallions," I comically stated to Jeraimy "we better head to Wall-4 before they stampede!"

"You're right," Jeraimy said chuckling while looking at the crew "I'll make the announcement." At that Jeraimy asked in a playful voice of someone who already knows the answer, "Hey team … Are you ready to tackle Wall-4 or do you need another break?"

Everyone was chuckling as their nearly simultaneous loud response echoed throughout C-three; "Take a break!"

"Gotcha," said Jeraimy, still with laughter-tears in his eyes. "I suggest we leave all the equipment where it is head to Wall-4 right away and find out if recovering the artifacts has changed its 'no admittance' policy." In full agreement the team rounded the dogleg and headed swiftly to Wall-4.

Wall 4 Return

As I negotiated the dogleg and saw Wall-4 unchanged from our first encounter, I was more than a little concerned. Obvious from the glances being exchanged by Jeraimy, Dyonne and Valerye who were walking together, they were also worried. Thus, assured they were thinking something similar, I said in a hopeful questioning tone, "Maybe I need to be right beside the wall before it responds?"

Surveying their faces, I could see they were no more convinced this was the solution than was I. Regardless, each grunted an unconvincing, "Perhaps?"

Even after my arrival at Wall-4 the vibrant shimmer presented by the previous three 'walls' remained absent. Instead, Wall-4's dull surface persisted: even when I placed my hand on it. Thinking Wall-4 may instead have a specific activation spot, I touched every part of what would be the Opening, but to no avail. As I continued efforts to coax Wall-4 'open' with the team intently watching my failed attempts, I remarked with concern to Dyonne, "Obvious from both the disenchanted looks on faces and the fretful remarks that the teams apprehensions are escalating."

"Yes, I believe your assessment is bang-on," agreed Dyonne. "However, I think I just might have figured-out what we need to do to have Wall-4 'open'," Dyonne stated excitedly! "Before I present my proposal to others, I would first like to get your feedback Divad," Dyonne coaxed.

"Sure," I responded "fire away," and then I thoughtfully added "but perhaps include Jeraimy as well as he is the expedition lead."

"Yes, correct again, thanks," Dyonne said as she signaled to Jeraimy to come over when finished speaking with Skilyem.

"What's up?" Jeraimy probed.

Dyonne said excitedly, "I believe I have a solution for 'opening' Wall-4, but I first want to run it past you and Divad, so I don't end up crushing more hopes."

"Wow … a possible solution … can't wait to hear the details," responded a now excited Jeraimy.

"I'm sure," Dyonne said to me and Jeraimy "you both recall my discourse regarding Divad's VibrationSignature as being 'key' to activating The-Bulges. Add to that 'key', the success Divad had retrieving the artifacts, which note only transformed for him," added Dyonne. "I believe The-Bulges perform like validators that somehow 'inform' following walls that those who accessed them are 'qualified'. I also believe the artifacts are not just fascinating trinkets but serve to enhance Divad's VibrationSignature when they are in his possession. If I am correct, Wall-4 will present its Opening only while Divad is holding the three collected artifacts," concluded Dyonne.

"Brilliant theory yet again Dyonne," Jeraimy complimented!

"Thank you Jeraimy," Dyonne said appreciatively and then asked "where are the three artifacts?"

"Divad is keeping them safe," Jeraimy responded.

"The artifacts are in my backpack," I rejoined "in the outer area with all the other equipment and items."

"Perhaps," suggested Jeraimy "we three should run the experiment before we involve others."

While Dyonne nodded affirmatively, I said, "Seems like the best approach - if it isn't the solution - to ensure no one gets more disheartened," then I added emphatically "but I am absolutely sure you are correct Dyonne!"

"Are you both up for a quick way to determine if I'm right or wrong?" said Dyonne confidently, and then added "Divad, can you stealthfully retrieve your backpack?"

"Definitely on both points," I said confidently as Jeraimy also nodded an enthusiastic yes!

"The experiment I have in mind," said Dyonne "will require you, Divad, to touch Wall-4 while holding the three artifacts. I'm postulating," Dyonne explained "the combined frequencies of the three artifacts will augment your VibrationSignature thereby producing a 'vibrational-key' compatible to Wall-4's frequency requirement."

"In summary then," said Jeraimy wistfully "if Wall-4 opens we're gold; if not we're slag."

"That's about the size of it," said Dyonne while she and I chuckled nervously.

Within about 3 minutes I returned; backpack in hand. I unwrapped each of the three artifacts, held them in my left hand, looked at Dyonne's and Jeraimy's nervous grins, walked the 5 remaining steps to Wall-4, and touched it. "Guess we're gold," I said with a mix of relief and excitement as Wall-4 had not only started shimmering a most incredible green but also produced a very appreciated opening!

"Oh my; oh my ... YES ... this result is incredible," said Dyonne excitedly "we must share the outcome with the team right away!"

"I for one am so glad," praised Jeraimy "you decided to be part of this team Dyonne: You have incredible deductive skills!"

Displaying abundant gratitude to Dyonne I said, "I certainly don't believe I would have ever figured-out the connections you devise so quickly and accurately."

"Thank you both," Dyonne responded with a mix of humility and delight!

"What say we three head back and present our good news?" suggested Jeraimy. To say the least, the team was ecstatic.

After about 5 minutes of watching our teammate's excited interactions and listening to their jovial chatter, Jeraimy addressed the group. "I suggest," said Jeraimy while making eye contact with each member until they quieted "... I suggest we grab our 'stuff', head into C-four, and as mid-evening is approaching in outside world time set-up camp for the night and depart for Wall-5 early in the morning."

"Additionally," Jeraimy continued without pause "once the encampment is established I recommend if C-four contains a Bulge-4 we procure whatever it may hold." Jeraimy inquired, "If everyone is OK with this plan let's reconvene at Wall-4 ASAP?" When no alternates were raised, each person quickly retrieved the items for which they were responsible and headed excitedly for Wall-4.

"I see everyone is here," I said "so time to open Wall-4." To ensure everyone was up-to-speed (before I touched Wall-4's surface) I briefly explained its unique requirements Dyonne had so amazingly deduced. When Wall-4 presented its Opening, the team was thrilled to go through and continue their extraordinary adventure.

"As with the previous caverns," Jeraimy interjected "please feel free to explore C-four for 15 minutes and then regroup near the position we expect to find Bulge-4."
After regrouping Jeraimy asked, "What did you folks find out about C-four?"

Jasone led with insights from his inspection. "Other than C-four's remarkable green hue, it is similar to C-three in both structure and dimension."

Scarlette quickly acknowledged aloud to the group, "You are correct Dyonne that C-four's outcropping or Bulge-4 is at the same relative coordinates as for previous bulges."

"One other tell, whose significance is perplexing to me," said Skilyem with a puzzled tone "is that C-four's luminescence continues the rainbow color progression of red, orange, yellow and now green.

"Thank all for your always keen and pertinent observations," Jeraimy said appreciatively and then added "are any other points or discussions outstanding?" None were offered.

Once camp was struck, the team gathered near Bulge-4 where Dyonne and Valerye were already finalizing setup of their reconfigured Spectrum Analyzer (SA). Shortly after everyone had arrived, Dyonne announced confidently, "As with Bulge-3, possible is our initial midline frequency/wavelength duo may not work. Don't worry though, as I am sure Bulge-4 will respond - as did the other bulges - to one of our eight combinations!"

"Even so, feel free to cross your fingers," Valerye inserted enthusiastically, "and as before do whatever else you believe brings luck!"

For this iteration Valerye was at the controls of the rejigged Spectrum-Analyzer. To ensure everyone's inclusion, she announced, "Dyonne, what is our first combination?"

Dyonne called out, "Frequency 566; wavelength 532."

Verifying the agreed setting was registered correctly, Valerye checked and confirmed the numbers and then declared, "Here goes!" While pressing the momentary-switch, Valerye counted out the requisite three seconds: "One ...; two ...; three ...!"

"Bulge-4 response negative," reported Dyonne ... "are you ready for the next combination?"

"I'm ready" responded Valerye. Ensuring everyone could hear, Dyonne called out the next values, "Frequency 516; wavelength 531."

After re-verifying the setting change, Valerye exclaimed, "Test number two now commencing." Valerye then pressed the momentary-switch while again counting out the three required seconds: "One ...; two ...; three ...!"

"Bulge-4 just responded," Dyonne announced excitedly! "Incredibly similar to previous bulges," Dyonne elatedly continued "Bulge-4 is emitting a striking green glow and has opened six flower-like petals! Okay Divad," Dyonne quipped playfully "your salvage skills are needed ... yet again ... best luck!"

Smiling mischievously I declared, "I'm reaching in to retrieve Bulge-4's currently nondescript 'stone' from its previously undetectable compartment." A few short nervous chuckles quickly yielded to silent anticipation. As for the three occasions previous, I firmly clutched the artifact. When it was safely out of its nest, I lightheartedly called out, "A-four has departed its Bulge-4 sanctuary! Within seconds after my retrieval, I added with amazement, "A-four's stone-like appearance just became translucent as did the first three artifacts!" I was definitely thrilled, as obviously were the rest of the now cheerfully chattering team members!

Jasone, who was once again intently scrutinizing the transitioned artifact still resting in my left hand, shared his always valued observation. "This artifact is also not totally clear; and much like the other artifacts, contains nine very, very thin 'threads' of different colors."

As all gathered around, Jeraimy stated appreciatively, "Thank you everyone for your valued input. Seems 'test four' has been passed as well," Jeraimy lightheartedly shared with everyone. He then added, "Get good rest as I'm sure the last two chambers will require some pretty hefty solutioning!" Jeraimy then extended his heartfelt appreciation, "Well done yet again everyone; outstandingly well done!"

"Thanks Jeraimy," I said with a tone that emphasized my deep respect for his knowledge and leadership "I will separately wrap 'A-four' and store it in my backpack's central compartment with the other three."

Wall 5

On my way to the breakfast 'table' I could see several folks already packing up equipment. "These vittles look fantastic," I exclaimed to Scarlette who arrived shortly after me!

"Yes," she agreed and added with a big smile "Gustovan likes to put on a show of his culinary talents when he's not practicing medicine."

"I had no idea part time chefing was one of his passions," I responded with surprise! "He is definitely excellent at it. Let's eat together and chat."

When Scarlette and I were close to finishing our meals, Jeraimy announced, "Could everyone meet at Wall-5 in thirty minutes?" He added, "Please bring all equipment and belongings as I am anticipating successful entry." Everyone sent a thumbs-up his way.

"Well," I chuckled softly to Jeraimy as we landed a few steps from Wall-5 "I see all are accounted for with 10 minutes to spare. You think perhaps they are excited for today's quests?"

"Perhaps they just didn't like the food," Jeraimy quipped back with his customary joviality. We both laughed heartily!

"Divad," asked Jeraimy in a factual voice, which disclosed he already knew the answer "do you have the four artifacts in your possession?"

"Yes I do," I said cheerily as I held them out for all to see. "Well then," continued Jeraimy "feel free to saunter over to Wall-5 and give it a feel!"

As I surveyed the faces of my silent teammates, each was staring at me anxiously; no doubt nervously eager for Wall-5 to provide its opening. "Here goes," I announced confidently. Absolutely incredible was to see Wall-5 morph from rock-like to a magnificent shimmering blue as I came close. A rousing cheer arose when a section of Wall-5 disappeared upon my touching it; notably much faster than one can say "open".

"I have to say," I stated loudly with a humorous lilt "I'm feeling a little like Aladdin must have when he breached the loot sanctuary of the 40 Thieves!" Lots of chuckles rolled through the team as each gathered their equipment and headed into C-five.

Everyone immediately headed toward the position where all believed Bulge-5 would be found. However, a few steps into C-five everyone halted abruptly. "Wow," I said loud enough for anyone to hear "C-five is obviously not configured like the previous two caverns: It looks huge!"

"Looks like C-five is not only much larger but also slants downward at about a 30 degree incline," stated a surprised Jeraimy "which will make foothold on the crystalline floor much more precarious!"

"Also," Dyonne noted as we all stood admiring C-five's splendor "in addition to C-five's expected blue luminescence, it is also sequentially pulsing each of the previous four caverns colors."

"Notably, not random pulsing," piped in Symtra "but as you can see, in broad circumventing bands that move from the entrance wall to some point far ahead."

"Fascinating … thank you," said an astonished Jeraimy "let's continue; shall we? However, as the descending slope up-tick may be challenging, let's all tie-off to one another with Divad and I leading … and please be careful," Jeraimy pleaded!

At that our tethered group moved carefully toward what was assumed to be the C-six wall. "Another surprise," I announced loudly "what we thought was the C-six wall is actually a constriction in what looks like a massive C-five bulkhead. Fortunately, it provides a long passageway with about the same opening size as C-fives entrance. Not only that, but I believe there is another section on the other side."

"You are correct Divad," said Skilyem. "My instruments measure this section as 20 metres long and 20 metres high. However, at 30 metres, it is two times wider than the previous cavern."

"Thanks Skilyem," said Scarlette "... C-five is definitely much larger! I suggest," advocated Scarlette "prior to proceeding into whatever is next, sensible would be to investigate this section for either Bulge-5 or any other anomalous features."

"Great idea," agreed Jeraimy "let's meet back here in 30 minutes." Upon regrouping, each person voiced their astonishment at C-fives enhanced characteristics.

"Just an indicator regarding the passageways dimensions," Jasone stated factually "it is 6 metres (about 20 feet) long with both a height and width of 3 metres (about 10 feet)."

"Great to know ... thanks Jasone ... OK folks, when you're all ready, let's re-tether and move forward," Jeraimy stated respectfully.

Just after the group exited the passageway, Skilyem announced excitedly, "The far end is not a wall either but another bulkhead with passageway. Seems we have landed in another section! Also, according to my instruments, it is dimensionally identical to the previous C-five section!"

"Astonishing ... thanks for the clarification Skilyem," pronounced Jeraimy who added "let's take 15 minutes to check this section out as well."

Upon regrouping, Dyonne - who also spoke for Scarlette and Valerye as the three had explored together declared "Although we did not locate a 'bulge' of any kind, we certainly found the crystalline characteristics of this section to be as astonishing as the first!"

"Astonishing for sure," I heartily agreed "however words do seem insufficient to describe the magnificence of our crystalline envelope. Not to worry regarding the bulge though," I continued "as Jeraimy, Skilyem and I did not locate it either! Hopefully The-Bulge we are anticipating will be in the section ahead."

After several others had contributed Jeraimy said appreciatively, "Thanks for your always keen observations everyone," then added "shall we re-tether and continue?" As nods and yups were unanimous, the group passed through the second 6 metre (about 20 feet) long passage and into the next section.

About five steps in Skilyem excitedly said, "Instruments are indicating a wall at the far end, which means this third section will conclude our C-five journey!"

Directing a question to Skilyem, Dyonne asked, "Is this section the same size as the other two?"

"Yes," Skilyem responded cheerfully "looks like all three C-five sections are basically identical in size, layout and structure."

"Good to know," Jeraimy stated supportively, then continued "as previously, let's take 15 minutes to check this section out!"

"How about that," Dyonne stated excitedly when all had regrouped "Bulge-5 is located in section-three after all, and in a position which imitates the locations of the other four chambers!"

Dyonne and Valerye dove right into their tasks of setting-up and configuring the Spectrum Analyzer for C-five's blue range frequencies: A challenging task due to the steep slope. "Let me remind everyone," assured Dyonne in a confident voice when all were clustered around "we have eight possible frequency/wavelength combinations in addition to our first midline choice. This means if Bulge-5 does not instantly respond don't agonize … I'm sure one of our combinations will be successful."

"As always," Valerye lightheartedly added "do feel free to cross anything you believe brings luck though!" Valerye, who was again at the controls of the reconfigured Spectrum-Analyzer asked Dyonne in a dynamic voice that ensured everyone heard, "What frequency/wavelength combination are we trying first Dyonne?"

"Trial one's midline combination," Dyonne responded "which is frequency 637 and wavelength 472."

After verbally confirming the numbers with Dyonne, Valerye rechecked to ensure settings were registered correctly, and then declared, "Here goes test number one!" As on previous trials, Valerye counted out the three required seconds while holding down the momentary-switch: "One …; two …; three …!"

"Bulge-5 response negative," Dyonne reported without worry "… next?" At Valerye's go-ahead, Dyonne called out the next iteration, "Frequency 636; wavelength 471."

Valerye again verified the numbers with Dyonne as she entered them into the registers. Once satisfied she, as before, counted out the three required seconds while holding down the momentary-switch: "One ...; two ...; three ...!"

"Bulge-5 response negative for trial number two," said Dyonne who added "next ... if you are ready?"

Trials three, four, five and six did not meet with success either. Obvious as the trials continued was that each failed attempt compounded the team's apprehension. At the sixth disappointment of nine possible trials, I noted to Jeraimy, "From the sound of the teams' rumblings, they are getting very restless; perhaps you could say a few words?"

"Good suggestion Divad," responded Jeraimy! "Hey folks ... recall at the start of these trials Dyonne and Valerye indicated one of the possible combinations will work. Note ... they still have three frequency/wavelength duos to test."

"Thanks for your support Jeraimy," Dyonne emphasized appreciatively! Valerye quickly confirmed with a 'thumbs-up' gesture just before she ran trial number seven. "Bulge-5 response negative for trial number seven," said Dyonne in a voice betraying her stress. I'm ready with the next frequency/wavelength combination. Bulge-5 response negative for trial eight of nine," reported a now noticeably frustrated Dyonne.

"Before the final trial," a concerned Valerye declared to the team, "Dyonne and I are going to run a diagnostic to ensure the equipment is not failing somehow. Give us ten minutes everyone." After slightly more than ten minutes Valerye announced: "The Spectrum Analyzer is functioning perfectly. Thus, we are going to proceed with the final trial."

At that Dyonne called out the last iteration, "Frequency 638; wavelength 473." Valerye verified, and requested Dyonne come over and re-verify the numbers entered into the registers. Once satisfied Valerye counted out the three required seconds while holding down the momentary-switch (I think her and Dyonne's eyes were closed): "One ...; two ...; three ...!"

"Ya HOOOO," Dyonne and Valerye excitedly howled in sync! "Bulge-5 just responded and it is emitting a magnificent blue glow," Valerye expressed with marked relief!

"Bulge-5," Dyonne chimed in "has also opened six flower-like petals!" The balance of the team crowded around Bulge-5 while cheerfully offering congratulations to Valerye and Dyonne.

"OK Divad," Dyonne said in a relieved voice "you're appropriation skills are needed once again!"

I was smiling very happily as I affirmed, "I'm retrieving Bulge-5's stone as requested! A-five's stone-like appearance" I excitedly continued speaking with amazement "just ... within seconds of its contact with my palm ... transformed to translucent: Just like the other bulge artifacts!"

As I was holding up A-five for all to see, I posed a question to Jeraimy, Dyonne and Valerye. "In that previous bulges were quick to respond, and Bulge-5 only responded on the last combination, do you think this was another test; perhaps of persistence or some such?"

"Wouldn't surprise me," said Dyonne: … "Me either," confirmed Valerye: … "Nor I," added Jeraimy!

Wall 6

"**W**ell crew," Jeraimy submitted warmly "who several weeks back would have reckoned we would be so close to our goal of accessing the sixth and final cavern?"

Knowing for sure the team did not need my instigation I asked nonchalantly, "Ready to tackle Wall-6?"

As a few were already heading excitedly toward the C-six wall while the rest were hustling to retrieve their gear response was minimal. Following the crews lead, I also reclaimed my backpack and the items I was assigned to transport and then headed toward Wall-6 as well.

As I drew to within about ten steps, Wall-6's appearance quickly morphed from stone-like into an amazing dance of Indigo and Violet colors that was doubly mesmerizing.

Jeraimy who was already near the wall remarked probingly as I approached, "This is the first time one of the walls has reacted before you touched it … any idea why?"

"I could take a wild guess," I said with a tone that showed I had little confidence in my notion. "Perhaps it's because I'm carrying all five artifacts in my backpack and we are standing near the wall?"

"As good a conclusion as any I have," Skilyem said as he apologized for eavesdropping.

"Everyone is waiting and excited to enter C-six," Jeraimy said enthusiastically "so if you are ready Divad feel free to touch Wall-6!" When an opening appeared, the team's spontaneous excitement was made unmistakable by their cheering, happy chatter, handshakes, hugs, back pats, and even a few wild dance steps! Jeraimy and I joyfully joined the impromptu celebration.

"It is great to see morale so high," I said to Jeraimy after about ten minutes of celebration. "I'm now really, really hankering to get into C-six and hopefully complete our primary mission. Also, I'm wondering whether C-six houses another bulge."

"I do believe," Jeraimy said emphatically "it is time to get those answers! OK everyone …; OK … everyone," Jeraimy repeated more loudly in order to grab everyone's attention "although I am enjoying our celebration, I believe an even bigger one is waiting for us in C-six. Shall we get our things, head in, and find out?"

Within less than three minutes the team was standing inside C-six. "It's almost surreal," said Scarlett "that we are actually in C-six. It is so incredibly magnificent!"

Dyonne added, "Yes it is," she heartily agreed "and thankfully its floor is not sloped … how wonderful is that! Also, I find this destination-cavern far beyond even the extraordinary of C-five."

"C-six seems so very much larger than C-five," I said to Skilyem who was standing next to me about 10 steps into the cavern.

"Definitely Divad … it's much more massive" responded Skilyem breathlessly! "My instruments peg its length at 140 metres (about 460 feet) - 50 metres (about 165 feet) more than C-five; and its height and width, which reckon to 40 metres high (about 130 feet) and 60 metres wide (about 200 feet), are double C-five's."

"Incredible," said Scarlette with awe "not just bigger but C-six's entire interior perimeter is encrusted with the most incredible material I have ever encountered or even imagined."

"Incredible as well is that even though at our present 1100 meter (3600 foot) depth, where darkness rules," Jeraimy offered with a voice laced with wonder "the caverns somewhat jagged elliptical interior perimeter is continually shimmering, shifting and strobing throughout the rainbow spectrum."

"Impressive," remarked an obviously mesmerized Gustovan. "Its striking luminescence once again precludes the need for supplementary light."

"Suddenly I'm feeling an enormous tsunami of gratitude," I said out loud to the group "for having been chosen to participate in this milestone sojourn with such notable scientist/explorers."

"Thank you Divad," Jeraimy said confidently "I'm sure I speak for everyone when I say you are equally appreciated. Let's check out our new digs for the next 30 minutes shall we?" said Jeraimy "and meet back here to discuss findings."

After team members had completed explorations and reassembled, everyone was eager to share experiences. Jasone was first to share. "Although larger, C-six seems to share a similar 'sectional' construction to C-five as all have no doubt also observed." Skilyem continued, "At present we are in the first section, which provides via its massive support arch a 5 metre (about 17 feet) wide by 10 metre (about 34 feet) long central passageway to another section."

"Just another quick update," injected Valerye "that neither Dyonne nor I located anything that might be Bulge-6."

After all had shared their observations Jeraimy said, "Well then, I presume its time to negotiate the passageway to wherever that leads." At that, everyone still excitedly chattering headed into and through the first passageway.

"Just to refresh everyone regarding the first constriction we are about to navigate," Jasone stated factually "it's opening provides 5 metres (about 17 feet) of both height and width, whereas its passageway is 10 metres long (about 34 feet), which notably equals the width of C-six's first arched buttress."

"Thanks Jasone … very useful … OK folks, when you're ready, let's continue onward," Jeraimy enticed respectfully.

Skilyem, when all had emerged from the passageway revealed, "My instruments indicate this is another identically sized section. Interestingly, the far end is not Wall-6 but another bulkhead with a similar passageway!"

"Thanks for the update Skilyem," pronounced Jeraimy who added "let's utilize the next 15 minutes to inspect this section."

Upon regrouping, Scarlette who indicated she was also contributing for her two exploration partners - Dyonne and Valerye - stated, "Although the crystalline characteristics of this section are equally as astonishing as those of section-one, there was no Bulge-6 to be found!"

"Neither did Jeraimy, Divad or I locate it," Skilyem reported, then added "hopefully The-Bulge we are seeking will be in a next section."

"Thank you all so very much for your observations," said Jeraimy appreciatively then added "let's continue shall we?" As one would expect, nods and yups were unanimous. Excitedly, the group negotiated their second 10 metre long passageway.

About five steps into the third section, Skilyem said, "Instruments are indicating a wall at the far end, which means section-three, will be the terminus of our journey."

Directing a question to Jasone, Dyonne asked, "Is this section also the same size and configuration as the other two?"

"Yes," Jasone responded cheerfully "looks like all three sections are very similar indeed."

"Thanks Jasone," Jeraimy said appreciatively then instructed "let's take 15 minutes to peruse this section!"

Upon regrouping, an excited Dyonne was first to share "The-Bulge is located in section-three after all. Not only that but in a position which mirrors the locations of the previous five chambers!"

"Before Valerye and I set-up and configure the Spectrum Analyzer for C-six's violet/indigo frequency ranges," Dyonne announced "I would first like to have a word with everyone! So … if all could gather around please?"

"Thank you everyone for assembling so quickly," Dyonne pronounced appreciatively! Valerye and I," Dyonne confided "previous to arriving in C-six conceived what we thought would be a rock-solid (if you'll excuse the pun) strategy for tackling Bulge-6."

"However," Valerye picked up the narrative "after seeing Wall-6 circulating two colors, Indigo and Violet, we have adjusted our approach. We are now postulating that the required frequency and wavelength must be either 'at' or 'near' the midline average of both those colors. Our caution is," Valerye continued "if our theory is not correct many dozens of combination-trials will be necessary. Point is, don't get worried if cracking Bulge-6 takes a little to a lot longer than the others … Okay?"

"As did the other bulges, we are confident Bulge-6 will respond," Dyonne concluded.

"Even though confident," Valerye added joyfully "feel free to cross anything you believe will fetch us luck!"

Valerye, who was again at the controls of the Spectrum-Analyzer asked Dyonne in a strong voice that ensured everyone could hear, "What frequency/wavelength combination did we decide to try first, Dyonne?"

"Trial one's midline combination," Dyonne responded "frequency 715; wavelength 468."

As Valerye had done at the other bulges, she counted out the three required seconds while holding down the momentary-switch: "One …; two …; three …!"

"Yes, Yes, Yes, Yes, and YES: First try," Dyonne exclaimed loudly. "Bulge-6 just responded not just by opening six flower-like petals but also rippling through rainbow colors like a kaleidoscope."

Everyone excitedly howled in sync and showered Valerye and Dyonne with sincere congratulations. "Divad," Dyonne said in a much relieved voice "you're unique aptitude is once again needed to secure the last artifact!"

"Happy to oblige," I responded enthusiastically! "Here it is," I exclaimed triumphantly as I held the A-six artifact high for all to see! So awesome to witness A-six's stone-like appearance transform to translucent," I stated gratefully and added "just like the previous five artifacts."

Big-Bulge

A credit to Urgency-team-2's professionalism," I commented appreciatively to Jeraimy who was gathering his requisite items "that everyone, instead of continuing celebrations has set to work executing their set of preparations for the next phase."

"I'm sure once C-six has exposed its marvels," Jeraimy responded with a big smile "the party will be unstoppable!"

Skilyem, Scarlette and Jasone (the team's three geological scientists) were focused on checking the calibration of a specifically fabricated frequency-Sensor that was earmarked to pilot investigations regarding the distinctive recurring pulses."

"The Frequency-Sensor, which was designed to locate the mysterious transmission we are seeking," Scarlette excitedly called out "has confirmed it is definitely emanating from somewhere within this section."

"The pulsing is emanating from over there," an excited Skilyem confirmed while pointing repeatedly toward a spot directly opposite section three's passageway "over there," he vigorously indicated "near the base of section three's far boundary."

Captivated, all moved swiftly toward the indicated location. "Unexpected, at least to me," I shared with Jeraimy as we arrived close to the designated spot that was already being investigated by the Geological team "that C-six contains a second much larger crystalline bulge. To me," I quickly added as I grappled for a reasonable comparative "it looks something like one-half of a one meter (three foot) exercise ball that's been blended onto the bottom part of C-six's otherwise uniform perimeter."

"I like your description," responded Jeraimy who posited jovially "I wonder if C-six's 'exercise ball' has another purpose besides transmitting?"

"Excellent question my friend," I responded. While visually surveying the bulges façade, I asked Scarlette and Jasone who were gently tapping on its surface, "Can you verify something for me please?"

Both were quick to nod acceptance. "Sure," said Scarlette "what is it?"

"Either my eyes are tricking me in this ever shifting rainbow-luminescence," I said "or this bulge has a seam (I scribed the barely perceptible join with my finger) … about 75 millimeters (three inches) in from its amalgamation with C-six's perimeter."

At that point Jasone rummaged in his backpack, which was near him on the 'floor', removed a very sturdy magnifying glass and proceeded to scour the area I had indicated. "I believe you are correct," said Jasone as he handed the magnifying glass to Scarlette "here … take a look."

"Good find Divad," confirmed Scarlette as she checked the entire surface of the bulge. "Definitely a seam … and it circles the entire bulge as well! "You're not just a pretty face after all," she snickered exuberantly.

"Nice to discover I'm useful for something," I rejoined with a mock chagrin that spirited Jasone to laugh even harder! When some composure was regained I postulated, "A seam must mean this 'bulge' opens as well: … yes; no? If you both agree, I believe our finding needs to be shared with everyone so they can help figure-out how to open it!"

"Absolutely Divad," agreed Jasone and Scarlette simultaneously! At this declaration I announced loudly, "Sorry to interrupt your pursuits, but we really need everyone's assistance." Within minutes the balance of the team gathered round the large bulge. Once we had shared what we knew and answered team questions, all were on-board with devising a way to coax it to open.

Dyonne was first to share her and Valerye's scheme. "So far, as all know," Dyonne summarized "the other bulges responded to frequencies within their specific color range. Thus," Dyonne continued "we postulate this bigger bulge will also."

"However," Valerye picked-up the narrative "as C-six presents a shifting array of all the previous caverns frequencies or colors; we are hoping to open this bulge by transmitting the midline frequency of red through violet. However," Valerye warned "a significant challenge could arise if this bulge does not open when bombarded by our midline frequency/wavelength. If Dyonne and I must resort to trialing combinations as was needed for Bulge-5," Valerye pointedly cautioned "our task will become exponentially more complex because possible cavern color combinations are enormous. Therefore, trial-and-error attempts could require days!"

"Thank you both for your excellent explanation," complimented Jeraimy. "Unless others have objections," Jeraimy said as he surveyed the crew for dissenters "you two should immediately proceed with your experiment. How long do you require to set-up to try the midline frequency/wavelength burst?" Jeraimy inquired.

After a two minute consult with Valerye, Dyonne replied, "About thirty minutes."

"Let us know if you need an assist," offered Jeraimy on behalf of everyone "and also, when you two are ready to initiate the frequency burst … I'm sure the team will want to attend."

"Yes, of course," chimed Dyonne cheerfully "we wouldn't want anyone to be absent when Big-bulge responds to our 'stimulation'."

"Thanks …," Jeraimy responded while chuckling at her innuendo "excellent!"

"While Valerye and Dyonne are readying their plan," Jeraimy declared "let's continue to brainstorm solutions in case their scenario is not successful." At Jeraimy's suggestion, the six remaining members of the team seated themselves in a circle.

"I and both Jasone and Scarlette would like to point out, said Skilyem confidently "that the Spectrum Analyzer is not the only generator of frequency that has enabled our arrival at C-six! Divad," said Skilyem as he pointed directly at me "both your VibrationSignature and the recovered artifacts have played most significantly in our success thus far."

"Therefore," said Scarlette after Skilyem offered her the 'floor' "we think it very likely that the Spectrum Analyzer will not work."

"Instead," Jasone continued after Scarlette concluded "what we believe is the artifacts frequency or frequencies - in some kind of as yet unknown union with Divad's VibrationSignature - will be the solution that reveals whatever we are assuming is inside the large bulge."

Speculations continued until Dyonne's flamboyant announcement cut through ongoing discussions, "We are ready to test our theory!"

"Feel free to cross anything you believe will fetch us luck as it has before," Valerye stated in her very optimistic tone!

Spectrum-Analyzer controls were being handled this time by Dyonne who asked when everyone had assembled,

"Valerye … what is our target frequency/wavelength trial combination?"

"Trial one's midline combination," Valerye responded "is frequency 195; wavelength 185."

While holding down the momentary-switch, Dyonne nervously counted out the three required seconds: "One …; two …; three …!"

"Sorry Dyonne," Valerye stated sadly "Big-bulge did not respond in any way!"

"Very unfortunate," returned a shaken and dismayed Dyonne "I really thought our postulate was correct. Have you folks brainstormed any alternate Plan-B's?"

"Yes," Jasone responded "in the off-chance your plan didn't pan out we did conceive a feasible alternate while you two were doing your diligence with the Spectrum Analyzer."

"Our alternate," injected Skilyem "actually incorporates the same 'frequency-is-the-key' premise as yours, except we believe the frequencies needed to open Big-bulge (as you have aptly labeled it) will be provided by some combination of Divad's VibrationSignature and the six gathered artifacts."

"Your idea definitely makes sense," Dyonne verified as Valerye nodded her approval as well. "Seems reasonable," Dyonne continued "as gaining access to the artifacts in the first place required the collaboration of everyone's knowledge and experiences."

"I am sure," interjected Valerye excitedly "this is just one more test to ensure we are worthy of whatever wonders C-six's Big-bulge is harboring!" While chuckling and chattering at the idea of having worthiness assessed once again, all nodded agreement with Valerye's assessment.

"Now," said Jeraimy heartily "all we need to do is figure out how to apply the idea!"

"Well folks," Gustovan articulated cheerfully as he re-joined the group "my suggestion is we eat while we debate next best steps. In that I have no-one to fix, and as most know, love to chef, I have prepared and laid out food just over there," he pointed.

"Huge thank you Gustovan; very special indeed," Jeraimy said appreciatively while everyone else thanked him as well. "Let's reconvene here in about 30 minutes, if that's Okay?"

When all had reassembled with their selected repast from Gustovan's exceptional food array, Jeraimy stood and presented his take on how to proceed. "In that Divad and the artifacts seem to be pivotal to providing the frequencies we believe will work," Jeraimy said thoughtfully "we should convene at Big-bulge once all have eaten, to figure-out what will inspire Big-bulge to do whatever it does."

Although everyone nodded appreciation of Jeraimy's idea, simultaneous passionate voices evidenced multiple other speculations were hankering to be presented.

"Once again, thank you so much Gustovan for the excellent repast," Valerye declared as the group was regrouping at Big-bulge. "So, who desires to share their idea of best next steps?" said Valerye inquisitively. As most spoke simultaneously, she added "one-at-a-time please." Within about 20 minutes of sharing ideas consensus was reached.

Dyonne provided the details of the agreed trial. "Divad will bring the artifacts to Big-bulge, and then, one at a time in bulge number order, place them on the cavern floor in front of Big-bulge: If that does not work then along its upper surface."

"I'll be back in a jiffy," I said to the group "just going to get my backpack! Sure glad I catalogued the artifacts by the cavern in which each was found," I said audibly on my return "otherwise executing our plan would be a whole lot more complex!" Everyone watched intently as I removed the individually wrapped and numbered artifacts from the sanctuary of my backpack and numerically spread them on the floor of C-six at the foot of Big-bulge.

"This is my first opportunity to see all the artifacts at once," Gustovan said admiringly "they all look identical to me."

"Wow," I said to Jeraimy with surprise as each member of the team meticulously assayed each of the six artifacts "Gustovan's statement certainly up-ticked everyone's inquisitiveness!"

"No kidding," Jeraimy agreed enthusiastically!

"Obvious," Scarlette pointed out once they were placed as suggested "is the current positions of the artifacts have no influence on Big-bulge."

"Let's proceed with the next possibility," suggested Dyonne and added respectfully "if all agree?"

"Here goes," I said with excited hopefulness as I began placing each of the six artifacts from left-to-right along Big-bulges upper surface while sequentially calling out their designation and effect!"

"A-one … no change, A-two … no change, A-three … no change, A-four … no change, A-five … no change, A-six … no change!"

"Well, well …," Jasone said with significant dismay in his voice "that's definitely disappointing! Let's not be deterred though, but keep working the problem my brilliant scientific friends," coaxed Jeraimy! "A solution must be possible as we have after many trials successfully arrived in C-six!"

"Perhaps," I proposed tentatively "if I gathered up the artifacts and placed them from right-to-left instead?"

"I will take the crews nods and shoulder gesticulations as a yes," I flamboyantly stated aloud. I began sequentially removing the artifacts from their perches on Big-bulge and placing each on the palm of my left hand. After placing A-three on my palm I became aware of a mild tingling sensation. Triggering interruption of my retrieval efforts was the pronounced tingling I experienced after putting A-four in my left hand.

I assume I hesitated longer than I thought because Jeraimy asked, "Is everything OK Divad?"

"Not sure," I said tenuously "as my hand just had a weird tingling spasm; not to worry, it's gone!" At that explanation I unceremoniously scooped both A-five and A-six with my right hand, and put them on my left palm with the other four. Wow," I exclaimed piercingly "the tingling sensation I thought was probably caused by a pinched nerve, just more than doubled!"

I was immobilized as I viewed the six artifacts rapidly blending into one seamless, nearly clear, egg shaped and sized piece: Tingling however had stopped. As I surveyed the fused artifact, I stated more loudly than needed, "The interior of the merged artifact contains nine almost imperceptible colored filaments; and they traverse its entire length." Hesitantly, as if to seek confirmation I was not delusional, I held out my trembling hand for all to view the now fully integrated artifact: Shocked, mesmerized and speechless described everyone.

I have no explanation, but I was somehow compelled to immediately touch Big-bulge! A gasp burst from everyone as the front portion of Big-bulge disappeared like The-Walls, to reveal an elliptical canister-like 'capsule' inside approximating the shape of a large mostly round watermelon.

Disclosure by Big-bulge of this next remarkable object, which everyone suspected had been sequestered within its inner sanctum for millennia, felt so utterly surreal no-one moved or hardly breathed for several minutes!

Dyonne was first to speak. "Seems 'opening' Big-bulge required not only Divad's VibrationSignature but also his concurrent contact with the six merged artifacts, which if all agree, I would like to name, TIFA: The middle four letters of 'arTIFAct."

"I for one think your label is excellent," complimented Jeraimy with an approving chuckle as he swapped amazed gazes between TIFA and the 'capsule-artifact' nestled in the loins of Big-bulge.

Although still dazed from Big-bulge's stunning 'reveal', I managed to stammer, "Anyone else notice the 'capsules' exterior appears composed of the same mysterious somewhat pliable material as the walls of C-six?"

"Yes," responded Skilyem. "However, even though the 'capsule' shimmers like C-six's roughish perimeter its surface is instead perfectly smooth; not jagged."

Sting

Each astounded colleague strived to grasp the implications of currently revealed events by scrutinizing both Big-bulge and its sheltered 'capsule'. After about 10 or so minutes, Dyonne was first to break the crews contemplations, "The 60-second interval pulses," she enthusiastically confirmed "are definitely being discharged from the 'capsule' inside Big-bulge!"

"Perhaps as was decided with the six bulge artifacts," Scarlette stated eagerly "the capsule should also be removed! Being able to see and handle the entire 'capsule'," she appended "would certainly foster improved analysis."

A short group discussion of Scarlette's next best-steps suggestion resulted in full agreement; however, with one supplement. "I feel our team lead, Jeraimy," Gustovan advocated "should have the privilege of removing the 'capsule' from its crystalline perch." All immediately agreed.

"Thank you so much for this honor," Jeraimy stated appreciatively while ensuring eye-contact with each person. "However, before proceeding to Big-bulge,"

Jeraimy confirmed, "I would like to underline that procurement of this 'object' will be a landmark accomplishment for us all! This is an amazing opportunity: Thank you again, one and all!"

Everyone intently watched Jeraimy's toils to remove the capsule. "Not possible," Jeraimy finally confirmed in an exasperated voice "no matter how vigorously I tug at the capsule, it will not budge … even slightly!"

An obviously disappointed Jeraimy probed, "Who would like to try next?" At Jeraimy's challenge each of the other six core members of UT-2 tried to remove the capsule: All without success.

After a short group debate, team consensus was delivered by Skilyem. "As the capsule seems immovable, it must somehow be either attached to the floor of the compartment or totally integrated with it."

After another brief team confab, Scarlette, our world-class Geologist turned her attention to me and expressed in a strikingly dispirited voice, "The team agrees Divad that it's your turn to have a go at capsule extraction."

"Okay … thanks," I acknowledged dispassionately "your offer is appreciated. However, after watching all your futile attempts to extricate it," I added with what the team must have concluded as pessimism "I'm sure my attempts will also be unsuccessful!" Hoping to lighten the downcast mood, I comically stated while walking to Big-bulge "maybe I should do some warmups before I try … Any suggestions?"

Everyone laughed! Levity was at its peak when I flamboyantly declined several "choice" warmup options that had been impishly offered. "No time like the present," I stated with zeal as I firmly gripped the capsule; then heaved vigorously!

"Yow," I involuntarily blurted as I careened backwards in dazed surprise! Next thing I knew I was on my butt with surprised faces staring down at me because the capsule was now firmly in my grasp! "The capsule," I blurted my astonishment "gave way as if not attached at all!"

"Clearly," I stated with wonder "I'm apparently not the only one totally staggered by this 'Excalibur-like' occurrence!" As I stood up checking for cuts from my tumble to the caverns rough floor, I announced, "Fortunately, no injury!"

"I'm going to place the capsule," I stated matter-of-factly "which I estimate at about 10 kg (22 pounds), on the floor next to Big-bulge. Fitting," I respectfully indicated to Jeraimy as I regained composure "I believe you as team-leader should have first access to the objects secrets."

"Thank you," Jeraimy said to me as we both checked for team endorsement. As it was evident all were in favor, I retrieved the capsule so I could ceremoniously hand it to Jeraimy. Feeling confident as all had agreed he should have the honors, Jeraimy said, "Thanks again everyone," and then reached to take the capsule from my hands.

Startlingly, when the capsule was within half an arm's length of Jeraimy's outstretched hands, a crackling sound quickly followed by a discharge resembling a barely visible lightning bolt shot out toward him and connected with several of his closest fingertips.

"Ouch and ouch," Jeraimy groaned while rapidly recoiling and shaking his jolted hand "that discharge really hurt!" Everyone, including me who was still holding the capsule was staggered by this unforeseen attack. Not wanting to be zapped as well, I gingerly put the capsule on the cavern floor and then quickly moved well away.

Dyonne, who was not one to be easily dissuaded or intimidated said, "I'll try next, if that's OK with everyone?" As unanimous 'go ahead and go-for-its' were proffered, Dyonne moved fearlessly toward the capsule: When close, she was also zapped.

Dyonne expressed that, "Being struck by the capsules discharge was like being besieged by dozens of simultaneous bee stings!" Due to her amusing assessment, which Jeraimy especially deemed fitting, team humor voted the capsule should from that point onward be known as "**Sting**".

Over the next minutes each team member took turns very cautiously approaching newly dubbed Sting. Sensibly, each team member heeded the warning 'crackle' on close approach, and quickly backed away from Sting before it spit its painful discharge.

Delivered by Valerye was what I considered a rather frivolous group consensus. "Divad," she said "the team agrees it's your turn to pick-up Sting."

I quickly responded utilizing a significantly grim tone, "I'm not a fan of that idea ... especially after observing Jeraimy's and Dyonne's painful outcomes. Just to be clear though," I added "I am going to back-off as soon as Sting crackles its warning." Surprisingly, I was able to handle Sting without any issues! Including me, everyone was flabbergasted by Stings' passive 'acceptance (???)' of my handling it.

Jeraimy delivered the teams invite: "As other options are unavailable anyway," Jeraimy stated conclusively "the team is unanimously requesting you be Stings custodian; at least until our three day return journey restores us to the relative comfort of our Antarctic lab."

"Happy to take on the Sting-sitting role," I said laughing! Everyone else laughed as well!

"Although our UT-2 exploration strategy was to remain in C-six for two days and collect material samples," Skilyem articulated "seems that option is unavailable as my Geologist associates and I have been unable to retrieve even a small piece of C-six's material."

"Therefore," Skilyem continued "I suggest an early departure back to the Antarctic base," after which he entertainingly added "and let's not have anyone else drop into an icy crevasse, Okay?" All laughed again as they nodded and voiced agreement that departure was the only practicable decision.

"Seems reasonable," confirmed Jeraimy "as C-six's unyielding crystalline walls have completely denied any intrusion, even from our very sophisticated diamond cutters!"

Sting was no more personable to the rest of the researchers at the Antarctic lab; nor, once I returned to the home research facility several days later with Jeraimy, Skilyem and Dyonne, to any of the staff in its facilities either.

Thus, as a consequence of Stings inexplicable acceptance of me, I was convincingly entreated (cajoled actually - by full access to all lab and staff resources) to figure-out what Sting and TIFA were all about. I jumped at the opportunity … of course!

Delving

Being unsure about the scope, method or likely duration of my Sting and TIFA investigations, I created a preliminary list of points that seemed (at the time) most crucial to resolve.

- What are Stings and TIFA's purpose(s)?
- Of what material(s) are Sting and TIFA composed?
- Do the 'caverns' with their elaborate material have other purposes? (If any; and if they are caverns at all?)
- What, if anything, does Sting contain: (I have a strong hunch it must house something due to not only its weight, size and shell composition but also the complex environment in which it was located)?
- Why am I the only one 'allowed (???)' to pick-up and handle Sting?
- How am I to understand something proven to be so impervious?
- What are Stings origins (Earth; not Earth???)
- And many, many etcetera's to be added!

I determined that endeavoring to locate evidence of similar DeeGe incidents would be a beneficial starting point. My strategy was to quickly scrutinize both classified and open reports and then further distill those that were pertinent. Little did I realize perusing decades of information would be so engrossing: The volume to be investigated was so great that my first few weeks skipped-by as if only a day. Unfortunately, I found nothing, absolutely nothing with useful similarity.

Due to Sting's acceptance (?) of me, my only distractions occurred when I was solicited as intermediary when team experiments required proximity to Sting. After a few days of serving as team liaison, Lab folks humorously dubbed me "Worker-bee". A fitting title they reckoned as I was the only one who could "buzz" in close to Sting without being "stung". I considered their witty label a compliment!

For three weeks and two days Sting and TIFA remained impervious to every methodology the Analysis-team's brilliant minds could conceive. Even though they were vigorously poked, prodded, drilled, frequency scanned, chemically assaulted and subjected to uncountable aggressive tests and procedures, they steadfastly withheld their mysteries unscathed.

About two weeks into the Analysis-team's research, while on another of dozens of Worker-bee assists, I commented to Skilyem, the research teams lead, "Great that Sting doesn't seem to mind being moved around into different laboratories by the mobile grappling-sling apparatus your team devised."

"Definitely a good thing," Skilyem responded with a sincere smile and chuckle "however, even with our precautions Sting has crackled-out its warning on multiple occasions. Graciously no one else has been 'zapped'; … not so far anyway," he added with a grin!

When a little more than 3 weeks had elapsed, Skilyem entered my lab. "Divad," he said with a slightly disheartened tone "Analysis-team specialists have not only exhausted every standard test but also run as many concocted alternate techniques as could be hatched: Unfortunately without even slightly useful results. I therefore invite you to re-claim Sting and TIFA," Skilyem continued with a smidgen of optimism in his words "in hopes you will uncover their secrets!"

Eager to defer some of Skilyem's despondence I declared, "Unlikely I will be any more successful than your amazing team."

"As you were THE key to not only accessing the six caverns and The-Bulges but also procuring Sting," Skilyem articulated courteously "I am betting your, let's call it 'relationship' with these 'items', could very well provide access to their bounties."

"I truly hope you are correct," I said without conviction, then thoughtfully added "I would appreciate having conversations with each colleague before I begin working with Sting and TIFA … if that's OK?"

"I figured you would," said Skilyem matter-of-factly "they are all prepped and ready when you are."

"Thanks Skilyem …," I stated as we continued heading toward the lab complex "I'll start right away," and then added my assurance, "also I'll keep you and the team well apprised."

"Much appreciated," Skilyem responded gratefully.

Completing detailed discussions with Jeraimy, now the facility's director, as well as with each member of the Analysis-team, which I learned had been shortened to just A-team, required two extended days.

On the morning of the third day I entered the lab currently housing both TIFA and Sting, pocketed TIFA, released Stings' harness and with bubbling anticipation liberated Sting into my two waiting hands. On the way to my laboratory, I could not help being thoroughly re-captivated by Stings unique exterior. Arriving at my lab, I headed to my workbench, sat down, and as I was manipulating Sting, which I had placed on my lap, I pondered out loud, "What next I wonder?"

Hardly five seconds had lapsed when Sting began emanating a barely audible, low frequency and oscillating sound - somewhat like a contented cat's purr - that was accompanied by a vibration, which sent undulating tingles down each leg. Surprise about Stings purring and vibration however quickly morphed to incredible excitement when Sting began slowly opening from multiple previously invisible seams and then into colossal astonishment when Sting began to slowly unfurl what, due to shape similarity, I dubbed "petals"!

"Analogous to the openings of The-Bulges," I too loudly confirmed to myself! Continuing my solitary conversation I concluded, "To complete its transformation obvious much more space than my lap is going to be necessary!" Consequently, I quickly relocated Sting to the center of my workbench.

As unfurling continued, a tapered, crystalline tower-like prominence was visible at Stings center, which I straightaway decided to tag "Central-Spire". Now fully visible I hesitantly muttered, "It certainly looks fully integrated with Stings encasement."

"Also, due to Central-Spires complex surface features," I continued my fragile theorizing "I'm deducing it some sort of control mechanism." Driven out of desire to gather proof, I suddenly felt compelled to touch the Central-Spire. As I ran my fingers over Central-Spires form, Stings outer shell began pulsing with the same mesmerizing colors as did the unknown C-six material on which Sting was perched several weeks previous: Then in about 15 seconds, seven crystalline petals were fully deployed.

"Unfurled Sting seems much larger than I thought possible," I said as I continued my monologue "thus, a useful next step would be to measure it. Sting," I said after completing measurements "you have just presented another enigma! Your 39.4 inch diameter (about one meter) calculates to a circumference of 123.6 inches or 3.14 meters, which closely equals the significant value of 'pi'! Is that a coincidence or purposeful?" I questioned out loud: "If intended, then for what reason?"

I was totally beguiled yet again, when each 14 inch (about 356 millimeter) petal began shimmering a different rainbow color. "The colors," I remarked to my empty lab "look identical to those strobing so magnificently within and across C-six's facade.

"Wow, another surprise," I stammered when bright circular points appeared from locations near each petal tip. "And another," I said excitedly when within seconds of these activations seven uniformly positioned locations just above the horizontal meridian of Central-Spire also lit-up!

I was rendered momentarily inert from surprise when directly above Stings Central-Spire appeared a flawless, very real looking holographic projection of Sting. "Amazing," I muttered as some composure was salvaged "the projected image is nearly indistinguishable from the way unfurled Sting currently looks on my lab bench!"

An electrifying realization twigged while I viewed three movie-like holograms re-cycle every 60 seconds! "Crystal clear to me," I asserted to Sting "you are presenting the beginnings of a very sophisticated Holographic owner's manual! Positively you are not of this Earth!" Spawned by these startling comprehensions was a disorienting mix of excitement, fright, apprehension and curiosity.

In that moment I resolved to not share my "alien" assessment with anyone. "At least," I thought aloud "until Sting relinquishes greater understanding of its offerings and purpose."

"Your first few strategic demonstrations," I said to Sting with a strong sense of keenness "have served to inspire my approach! I pledge to decrypt the teachings of each holographic presentation to honor the sentient entity that has gone to such impressive lengths to deliver to our world what I'm expecting will be momentous knowledge!"

Emergence

To ensure my Sting and TIFA investigations remained uninterrupted (at least for now), I would curtail access to my lab by tagging it "NO-entry". Of course a believable justification of my action was essential to allay any chance of A-team feeling alienated.

Thus, at our first debrief the next morning I explained my position. "I believe prudent to ensure everyone's safety from any Sting countermeasures is to quarantine my lab," (although I knew my memorandum was only a nugget of my much broader objective). Conveniently, as all had viewed OU-2's "lightning" videos, my proposal was accepted without resistance.

I humorously thought to myself: I'm positive that Sting will dissuade anyone else from interacting anyway - either assertively by a "lightning" zap or passively by simply closing up!

Immediately after our meeting I retreated to my lab and began working my plan. So my chronicles would be of best quality, necessary first was to verify that the labs audio and video equipment were functioning properly. Once confirmed I dictated, "The first holographic image, which I hereby tag HoloVid-1, is my starting point. As it flawlessly depicts a fully deployed Sting, descriptive detail is unnecessary."

"Following HoloVid-1 by about ten seconds," I continued verbalizing "a more detailed HoloVid-2 presented. With about a six times magnification, the rendering highlights a small zone, which is located near the junction of the green petal and the Central-Spire base. As the indicated zone is emitting an identical green to its corresponding petal," I conclude that "its matching green color is not a coincidence."

"Although clear," I continued "that Sting is guiding my attention to this zone; exact features remain rather nondescript at my current distance. Thus, I have moved close to Sting and am cautiously moving my hand toward the green zones position. Amazingly," I added excitedly "when about a finger-length away from the target, it lit-up, thus clarifying its detail. Also, each time my hand is withdrawn the zone dims; but when close, it brightens!"

"Absolutely fascinating," I voiced to any otherworldly entity that might be listening. "I'm actually interacting with your Alien technology. I'm amazed, awestruck and intensely excited," I acknowledged as I regained momentum "regarding what disclosures might be next on Sting's agenda!" As if Sting heard me while I was admiring Stings shimmering crystalline splendor, HoloVid-3 displayed.

"HoloVid-3," I stated to the automated documenter "just initiated by replaying the first two HoloVids. Additionally however, a small spot in the Green-zone is depicted as much brighter. I believe," I continued detailing "Sting is directing me to touch this particular Green-zone spot, which is about the size of my finger tip."

"As I have no fear of any punitive action," I stated confidently "I am going to touch the specified spot. Noteworthy," I reported "is that the entire Green-zone brightened as my hand approached. Intriguingly, when I touch the target spot it not only substantially brightens but also imparts a slight tingle to my fingertip!"

"Interestingly," I continued my recorded monologue "the Green-zone did not dim-out this time but stays half illuminated as do the other eleven variously hued Green-zone spots. I figure these will turn out to be control buttons. Also, now easily visible is the Green-zone's compact shape, which resembles a symmetric petal that swoops gracefully up from the base of the Central-Spire."

"I'm convinced that Green-zone button arrangement is purposeful," I resumed commentary "with four buttons across the 'petals' widest part; three above and three below; and one centered above and one centered below, which is the one I touched. Additionally," I continued my detailing "each Green-zone button is slightly inset, which results in buttons being bordered by a minimally elevated, narrow, smooth meridian or ridge. Furthermore, the outer perimeter of the Green-zone is not only slightly textured but also marginally higher than the ridges of its enclosed twelve button array. I'm sure Sting will clarify why button features are so unique."

"HoloVid-4 just deployed," I specified "and added one extension to the HoloVid-3 presentation: Both the bottom and the top Green-zone buttons are lit. As I am becoming familiar with Stings coaching," I added "I am going to simultaneously touch both buttons. The outcome makes clear," I continued "these two buttons turn Sting full-on because the Central-Spires other six zones, which are each positioned above their correspondingly colored petals, just lit-up as well! Green for ON makes sense," I commented to Sting with an appreciative chuckle. "Wonder if this is a Universe-H default or somehow specifically tailored for humans?"

"I'm going to present an educated guess," I stated "that each of the Central-Spires seven petal-zones, with each of their twelve correspondingly hued buttons enable extensive functionality. Undoubtedly these seven Sting Control-zones have been devised to facilitate what I calculate as tens-of-millions of interactive button combinations. I'm also positing that Stings crystalline structure is purposed to storehouse the enormous quantity of data hinted at by these extreme permutations?"

"I am feeling a deep sense of privilege that I was chosen to explore and hopefully disclose Sting and TIFA wonders. I'm anticipating," I continued my oratory "now preliminaries are concluded, that Sting will reveal many more secrets."

A gigantic yawn underscored I had been working non-stop for plus 18 hours. "Although I do not want to push the pause button on my Sting adventure," I stated aloud for recording continuity "I'm going to call it a day as attention deficit from fatigue is counterproductive."

"Well, well." I said as I stood up and readied to depart the lab "Sting just presented HoloVid-5. Although similar to HoloVid-4, instead the top and bottom Red-zone buttons are lit-up. As I am becoming familiar with Stings intentions," I uttered as another yawn pressed its way forward "I am going to push both Red-zone buttons simultaneously. How about that," I stated with amusement "I definitely do not need to worry about someone tampering with Sting while I'm elsewhere as Sting just folded itself up and returned to its impenetrable form."

On the trip home (and until I fell asleep an hour later) my mind was effervescing with prospects of what surprises might come next. In all my conjectures though, little did I realize the next few days would revolutionize not only our understanding of the design, function and scope of Universe-H and the role corporeal entities play in sustaining its robustness but also gargantuan sets of current understandings and perspectives.

Interacting

Due to my sprouting familiarity with Sting, I was feeling relaxed today: Burgeoning with expectation, yes; but unruffled as I watched team members assemble for our scheduled morning update. Brevity was my desire for today's session. Thus, I divulged only that Sting had presented five sequential instructional holograms that revealed ON and OFF controls.

However and not surprisingly, our team of apex scientists extended the time by posing many astute questions: My response to most, "Still working to clarify." Fortunately, their update regarding ascertaining the atomic composition of the caverns crystalline material was short because headway was negligible. When I excused myself, the team was chattering excitedly. I was smiling because I presumed their levity was due to the helpfulness of my responses.

When I entered my lab about fifteen minutes later, Sting remained as I had left it the previous evening: A round, slightly flattened stone perched on my labs workbench. As I approached, I mock quizzed Sting, "To activate you will I need to place you on my lap again?"

Surprise stopped me in my tracks about five steps away. "Wow, question answered," I exclaimed as Sting spontaneously unfurled in about 3 seconds! "Way, way faster than yesterday," I blurted uneasily!

As I continued my immobilized staring I stated too loudly, "Okay Sting ... I find three aspects unsettling! First, you seem able to 'recognize' me, second 'pinpoint' my physical position and third reinitialize when I approach! I cannot tell," I continued with bristling emotions "which is grander at this point, disturbing observance of your alien capabilities or fear of your seeming sentience!"

While struggling to retain some composure, I commanded myself, "Okay Divad, push past your concerns and pretend for now you are an old-hand at interacting with far advanced alien technology, and touch those two indicated green ON buttons. Again wow," I continued excitedly "Sting nearly instantly looks as it did yesterday just before I turned it off!"

"HoloVid-6 is day-two's first," I dictated. "It is presenting a much enlarged graphic of the Green-zone array on HoloVid-6's left half-section; whereas a likeness of Sting is being displayed on its right half-section. "Well it seems," I stated with enthusiasm "deciphering todays HoloVids is ramping-up to be more challenging!"

"A blinking green-button in the left-half of HoloVid-6," I continued "is the only noteworthy current activity: Specifically, the far right one of the four middle-row buttons."

"When I touched it, I detailed "the far left-button on the Green-zone's middle row blinked instead. Then when I touched it, HoloVid-6 slowly regressed to HoloVid-5. Now clear," I continued "is that the right-button performs as play/forward, whereas the left-button is spool back."

As day-two progressed, Stings HoloVids systematically served-up many additional Green-button functionalities: initiated by touching either a single button or combinations of two or three buttons. Also, I learned the simultaneous pressing of the upper and lower Green-zone buttons was not to turn Sting ON at all. Instead, this Green-zone button duo combination was provided only to access this series of introductory HoloVids.

For instance, HoloVid-26 indicated a three Green-zone button combination. When touched, displayed was what I assumed to be a comprehensive index: Presumed because the mega-list was in an unknown graphic language. As I perused its thousands of entries, obvious was Sting housed extensive knowledge archives, whose comprehension I estimated would require decades to examine and comprehend; once translated.

Even as I forced myself home for some much needed sleep I remained eager and enthralled. Electrifying thoughts on the drive home produced many wild scenarios of what Sting might next reveal. Turned out, even with all my wildly inventive fabrications, I truly had no inkling of the extreme marvels Sting was about to disclose on Day-three ... and beyond.

Although Stings remarkable Day-Two HoloVid illustrations dramatically both piqued my scientific appetite and sparked wonder and expectation, I would soon realize Day-Two disclosures were only preparatory. Stings HoloVid-27 would shatter both my reasonable-expectation list and my virtual catalog of most implausible possibilities.

Here's what happened after our morning update meeting where I disclosed some of yesterday's key happenings as well as my take on what I was expecting to occur in the next week or so!

Day-Three initiated more-or-less as expected with Sting tendering multiple HoloVids that identified many additional two and three button combinations. "No doubt these groupings," I thought out loud "will ultimately facilitate enabling all Stings functionalities." Unexpectedly however, when I was scanning my rough notes of the previous many HoloVids for omissions, Sting departed from what I had anticipated would be its step-by-step instructional trajectory of revealing single and dual-button functionalities.

Instead, HoloVid-28 brightened five buttons from three Central-Spire groups: 2-yellow, 2-green and 1-blue. Surprised at Stings deviation I exclaimed, "Well ..., as I'm pretty confident Sting is indicating the five highlighted buttons are to be touched simultaneously," I stated aloud while miming several possible finger arrangements "my theory that Central-Spire groups operate independently is toasted."

"Actually … after reexamination," I stated with renewed conviction "it's now obvious this button arrangement is not unintentional; but deliberate. I conclude this because are not only the five buttons conveniently situated but also the yellow, green and blue Central-Spire groups located next to each other! Here goes touching the five buttons," I uttered expectantly!

"Incredible! No question HoloVid-28 complexity has substantially up-ticked," I continued with amplified fascination "because Sting has rendered five distinct sections on an amazing translucent elliptical pallet, which surrounds both Sting and I at a distance of about 3 meters (about 10 feet)!"

"I'm concluding HoloVid-28's flawless rendering of Sting is the launch point," I stated confidently "because to the left of this section, which I am tagging 'section-1', is a right-pointing, pulsing arrow. Also depicted is a pair of parallel, acute angle, zigzag lines, which slightly overlap Stings green Central-Spire buttons."

"I must admit," I stated aloud "section-1's meaning eludes me. Nonetheless, I will continue describing the other four sections of HoloVid-28 in hopes that all will become clear to me. 'Section-2' depicts two closely placed horizontal and parallel dashed lines, each with seven rectangular segments. Interestingly," I continued detailing "every seven seconds the segments of the upper dashed line strobes in rainbow color order from left-to-right; whereas the lower dashed line segments strobe from right-to-left."

"Section-3, whose message I also cannot reconcile," I continued perplexed "shows what looks to me like a slowly rotating ball. Although Section-4 presents a second Sting rendering, it is not static, but instead quickly and repeatedly expands slightly and then reverts to its original size. Section-5 depicts blinking buttons: three green and three blue. Puzzling is that each button is identically positioned within its respective Central-Spire group: the top button, the bottom button and the left button on the middle row of four."

For the balance of the day I attempted to decipher the meaning of HoloVid-28's five sections. Even after precipitating wild scenarios, HoloVid-28's messages remained elusive. When progress was less than significant I resorted to pleading with Sting: "Can you give me a clue to your messages; because I'm stumped."

When that act of pointless desperation didn't work, I decided to call it a day. While driving home it twigged: Needed are additional brains. "Good time to engage A-team," I thought aloud "because presentation complexity will no doubt continue to escalate."

When I requested help at the next day's morning meeting, the entire team was excited to become involved with Sting once again. "I apologize," I said regretfully "that I allowed Stings temperament to dissuade my getting everyone engaged earlier!"

"Thank you everyone! I believe," I continued respectfully "although you will have ample opportunity to perform your own assessments, the first step should be to review my progress to date." When the team indicated consensus I explained, "Thus far I have viewed twenty-eight Sting renderings, which I call HoloVids. Of these twenty-eight HoloVids, the first twenty-seven lessons I found clear; whereas what HoloVid-28 wants to convey," I supplemented by a big shoulder shrug "remains a mystery to me."

"Respectfully," I continued "I request we begin the HoloVid-28 figuring-it-out process by your first watching and discussing each of the previous twenty-seven HoloVids." I then queried, "Does anyone have objections or alternates?" I was pleased when the team was unified in my approach!

"One more point before we begin," I said courteously to Jeraimy, Skilyem and Dyonne "I would like to introduce two new faces borrowed from the DeeGe team: Glorya and Symtra. They are replacing two other very competent scientists who have been asked to return to the Antarctic station and continue cavern research."

After about 15 minutes of introductions, Dyonne spoke up, "I know I speak for everyone that we five are anxious and ready to begin deciphering Stings messages!" Without hesitation, all six A-teamers, including me, nodded emphatic concurrence with Dyonne's proclamation.

Expectant and charged, A-team began its collaborative quest. As planned the first two days of the team's participation was dedicated to examining HoloVids one through twenty-seven, asking me questions, and engaging me to 'push' Stings buttons. We quickly learned as long as my A-team colleagues stayed at least two arms-lengths away, Sting remained user-friendly and continued HoloVid presentations.

"I wonder if at some point," queried Jeraimy with a mischievous tone loud enough to be heard by all "whether Sting will actually permit contact by others or remain dedicated only to Worker-bee?"

Laughing heartily at the resurface of the Worker-bee tag, I responded lightheartedly, "Wish I had an answer to your question Jeraimy," then soberly added "… I really do!"

At Day-three's morning meeting everyone in their own unique way reported being familiar with prior HoloVid presentations. "Today," I announced when everyone had shared their views "I would like us all to watch and hopefully begin to decipher what HoloVid-28 wants to convey."

Within a few moments of my initiating HoloVid-28, I announced, "I am distributing a folio to each of you, which details my take on HoloVid-28's five sections. Please note my intention," I articulated respectfully "is for this document to spirit discussions; not control them. As I pointed toward the front of the room I added, "Its contents are also displayed on the big screen."

"Thank you for your documentation," Symtra declared appreciatively "it is wonderfully comprehensive. How long do you believe Sting will keep HoloVid-28 viewable Divad?" Symtra asked with a trace of apprehension!

"I believe as long as we like," I responded courteously, then added chuckling "as long as everyone else maintains Sting-acceptable distance that is!" Several guffaws and cheerful retorts followed, all which gratefully lightened the mood.

"So …," Jeraimy kicked in thoughtfully "the non-Sting graphic in section-1, based on both its overlapping position as well as its jagged appearance, seems to me either a warning not to touch the indicated Central-Spire section or, and this is the one I choose, some sort of communication invite."

"Yes," said Skilyem excitedly "Glorya, Symtra and I are heading in the same direction as your favored choice; except we think more likely section-1's overlapping graphic is suggesting an interface of some type."

"I'm 99.99% sure," I said confidently "Jeraimy's 'warning' option can be ruled out as I have definitely touched every part of the Central-Spire without negative incident." When I noticed Dyonne fidgeting I asked in a friendly manner, "Dyonne … you are un-customarily pensive … what's up?"

"Thanks Divad … pondering I guess," Dyonne responded thoughtfully and then added "definitely on board with the communication idea as those double jagged lines look like they are meant to indicate frequency handling of some sort. Also," Dyonne added "as green always initiated some action in the first 27 HoloVids (great name by the way Divad) I'm postulating some button combination will be needed to DO whatever

Sting wants us to DO." Everyone nodded and articulated vigorous confirmations!

"First, thanks for the compliment Dyonne … much appreciated," I said warmly before asking "if it's OK with everyone, shall we continue with section-2?"

"Is it OK to jump in and share my current working hypothesis," queried Glorya nervously.

Jeraimy looked around at everyone's nods and said, "Seems all are fine with listening; so go for it!"

"Having read Urgency-team-2's reports, observing Stings HoloVids, contemplating Divad's 'sections' summary and intently listening to everyone's points," Glorya shared "my thinking keeps looping and pressing one deduction.

As you may know," continued Glorya "Dyonne, Symtra and I were jointly responsible for not only the conception of the communication functionality of the DeeGe satellite swarm but also overseeing its manufacture and deployment. With HoloVid-28, what I am seeing most certainly looks like a request by Sting to communicate," Glorya stated confidently "which probably means it has advanced beyond artificially intelligent to perhaps sentience. I suggest this from many additional indicators."

"Best guess," conjectured Glorya "is if we simultaneously push the six indicated buttons, Sting will somehow connect to our planets information web, upload what it needs, and proceed with whatever is next without asking. Issues are," Glorya summarized with a most serious tone "we neither know what Sting wants to communicate, nor whether Sting might be malicious once connected: Like an elaborate 'Trojan-Horse' designed to disrupt or appropriate an entire world!"

"Excellent points well taken," Dyonne said seriously "so, what is urgently needed is a way for us to determine if Sting is friendly or hostile!"

"Divad," stated Jeraimy questioningly "you look a tad distressed at the moment. Would you like to share why?"

"Yes … thanks Jeraimy," I responded appreciatively "I would like to tackle Glorya's concerns, which I agree require our most stringent due diligence to resolve prior to taking any additional action. Allow me spread my conjectures and facts on our virtual thought table first," I requested "then each of you add content to the 'buffet' until we agree every concern and possibility has been revealed."

"Looks like you have the floor," Jeraimy said after scanning faces for dissenters "or should I say 'buffet table'," he added humorously.

"Thanks everyone," I said respectfully while chuckling along with the others. "At this point … and I'm certainly open for correction as we proceed … at this point," I repeated "I'm plus 99% certain Sting is not anything like a Trojan-Horse but an amazing gift from Out-There somewhere! My reasoning, and bear with me," I stated energetically "is as follows. If Sting is a Trojan-Horse then why such an elaborate protection system of six impervious crystalline caverns that defy entry except via the combination of my VibrationSignature and artifacts gathered from The-Bulges, which as you recall were very challenging to acquire."

"Additionally," I continued "not only did the six artifacts have to merge in my hand and become what we call TIFA before Stings compartment would open but also Sting itself could not and will not be handled by anyone but me. Seems if malicious intent was at play, accessing Sting would be made as easy as possible; not made nearly impossible," I concluded.

"Thank you for sharing your very plausible argument for moving forward," said Skilyem kindly "however, although I could quickly agree with your reasoning, I believe we owe it to our planets inhabitants to be absolutely sure our determination is correct."

"How about this," Jeraimy said with purpose "let's do a round-table conversation of pro's and con's for the next 60 minutes; then revisit the question. I think all six of us must either be in full agreement to move forward," Jeraimy continued in a decisive tone "or we will continue to gather data until absolute determination can be made; one way or the other!"

With no protests, discussions continued for about two hours before Jeraimy requested a 'show-of-hands' vote. "Well let's find out," Jeraimy declared in his friendly booming voice "if we have a consensus on pushing the indicated buttons or not! If not in favor, please raise your hand," Jeraimy requested. "No-one? ... I guess we're a go then," Jeraimy stated excitedly! "Divad?" requested Jeraimy "will you please touch the indicated buttons."

"Happy too," I said without hesitation. However, as I was about to touch the buttons, I halted when I glanced at my fellow teammates and saw everyone quickly distancing themselves from Sting.

Although my first reaction was amusement, it was short lived. My cheerfulness quickly morphed to alarm sufficient to abort my action. My conclusion was immediate: The team must actually be fearful of the 'button-pushing' outcome. As I quickly scrutinized each face, I anxiously questioned, "Is everyone still in favor? I'm asking because of your hasty retreats."

Obvious from the team's verbal affirmations, nods, winks and thumbs-up, all were still in favor. Satisfied our plan was a unanimous GO I relaxed and re-positioned myself at Stings Central-Spire, then touched the designated button array. Sting instantly began emitting a very quiet oscillating hum while the five graphics morphed from static into animated.

"Incredible to see the five HoloVid sections activate," I said to the group with fascination lacing my voice!

"True that," responded Jeraimy: "fingers crossed that we made the correct decision!"

"Seems to me," I said with a chuckle in my voice "we have relied very heavily on 'crossed-fingers' these past weeks!" Chuckles rolled through the team.

As HoloVid-28's animations continued, team members excitedly chattered amongst themselves. However, as the ten minute mark approached, tone texture was noticeably betraying the groups growing apprehension.

Hello

At about the twelve minute mark Sting said in a pleasant sincere voice, "Hello ... I am interfaced with your worldwide information web and so we may effectively converse, have assimilated most languages."

Even considering all the amazing events experienced to date, no-one was expecting such an unprecedented occurrence. If physically possible for six 'jaws to drop' to the floor from shock, it would have happened right then.

"I have much to convey," continued Sting calmly "both in regards to what I am, as well as both my purpose and offerings. However, immediately imperative is to not only alert of significant off-world generated dangers triggered by my activation but also provide the means to thwart these planetary wide safety threats. Time is of the essence!"

"Also, from my assimilation of global information," Sting resumed over the teams loud and understandably anxious exchanges "I have determined for your and other species survival global-warming must also be quickly rectified. I will provide a relatively straightforward solution," Sting added "which has been effective for many other planets whose populations have made similar environmental blunders."

"As we must quickly deploy planetary defenses," Sting stated "I will answer your questions for the next thirty minutes only!"

Dazed, I blurted in what must have been an immensely confused tone "Thank you so much," then quickly added "I do have so very many questions!"

"Logical you are both mystified and curious Divad," responded Sting "likely similar for each member of A-team as well."

"You know who I am?" I said with stunned wonder!

"Yes," replied Sting "and all of your teammates as well. Since being activated by my extraction from what you quaintly term C-six's Big-bulge," Sting continued "I have not only pulled details pertaining to all A-team associates from your information systems but also preserved all conversations."

"No intended offense Sting," Dyonne injected curtly "but I could not help notice you use 'I' when referring to yourself. Do you consider yourself sentient?" she asked with an undeniably skeptical tone!

"Your cynicism is understandable Dyonne," responded Sting respectfully. "How about you and the team ascertain that once our critical projects are concluded?"

"Your proposal is certainly logical and prudent," rejoined Dyonne "and from the team nods, I see all are in agreement."

In an uncustomary high pitched and nervous tone that revealed Jeraimy's astonishment, he asked, "What …what should we call you?"

With an unmistakable chuckling sound that surprised everyone, Sting replied, "I do quite like the conferred 'Sting' moniker."

"OK then collaborator Sting," Symtra uttered probingly "three quandaries have been grinding me for resolution since your removal from Big-bulge: How did you come to be here on Earth; how long were you sequestered; and most perplexing, why is Divad the only one who can touch you?"

"I am eager to answer all your questions during deployment of our second project," Sting responded pleasantly "but first," Sting stated emphatically "and I cannot state this strongly enough, we must ensure planet safety very quickly!"

After a quick confab with the team, Jeraimy declared in a serious tone that underlined his appreciation of the planet-safety imperative presented by Sting, "What do you need of us?"

"The six caverns you solutioned your way through (and yes, tests they were) are far more than what they appear," informed Sting. "The first four are outposts tasked with planet protection, whereas what you term C-five and C-six link to form an interstellar vehicle. I and what you call TIFA," Sting continued "are essential to their integration and operation; as well as many other features, which will be revealed once the planet is secure."

"Quickly though, to provide some perspective," Sting offered "TIFA and I were created hundreds-of-thousands of your Earth years ago by extremely technologically and socially advanced, yet elusive entities called Kyorma'kren."

"Although surprisingly little is known regarding either their form or lifestyle," offered Sting "Kyorma'kren gifts of vastly superior technology have proven highly beneficial to many Life-Forms on diverse planets in many galaxies. Without exception," elaborated Sting "to be validated as deserving, each Species was similarly challenged as were you."

"Kyorma'kren technologies," continued Sting "endure as the only resources capable of tapping into and utilizing Universe-H's core power drivers: Gravitational waves and Quantum tunnels, as well as both micro and macro electromagnetic forces."

"Additionally, although the three known malevolent species have not yet replicated Kyorma'kren technology," disclosed Sting "one particular very ancient bloc, the Zqorsa-chyem's are continually striving to develop superior-to-Kyorma'kren capabilities. Thus, even though they operate mostly pilfered technology," elaborated Sting "Zqorsa-chyem developed capabilities are increasingly challenging to countermand."

"If I have your permission," requested Sting "I will commence deployment of C-one through C-four pods to designated LaGrange arenas. When established, activated and linked, I suggest their array be named 'Sentinel' as this is my closest translation of their purpose."

Sting continued, "C-one and C-two will be deployed to L1 and L2 respectively. C-three and C-four, as you correctly noted are double the length of either C-one or C-two. Once C-three and C-four arrive at L5 and L4 respectively, each will reconfigure into two bastions who's 'mates' will move to the 'poles' of the four Lagrange positions."

"As you are no doubt already aware Sting from your recent detailed examination into Mankinds current condition," Jeraimy said with a mix of sadness and angst "you no doubt have correctly concluded that Human generational dogmas are anything but integrated; more antagonistic actually!"

"Yes, I do understand many countries and corporate factions vigorously press selfish beliefs and conflicting agendas," responded Sting "however, none of that will matter because without Sentinels immediate deployment planetary species counts will shortly become zero!"

"Deployment of Sentinel," Dyonne stated in a mostly panicked tone "could very well trigger activation of hundreds of military forces … some of which will feel justified in nuclear response … thus obliterating us anyway!"

"My apologies for not informing sooner: I am still gaining familiarity with subtle language tonalities," Sting stated with what sounded like genuine regret, and then added "by exploiting the Earth's electromagnetic field, 'Sentinel' deployment will look-like and record as a short duration, freak Antarctic lightning storm."

"When the imminent attack occurs," Sting continued credibly "all Earth factions will be thankful for your teams' actions that saved both them and the planet!"
"Sounds like a slam-dunk to me," Jeraimy animated to the group "first ensure Earth is safe; then ask permission to assemble an oversight committee ... All in favor?" All hands followed Jeraimy's into the air. "OK Sting," said Jeraimy with authority "proceed with Sentinel's launch!"

In less than ten minutes reports began pouring in from various Antarctic posts. All descriptions similarly detailed a unique, bright and active three minute lighting event that encompassed the magnetic South Pole. When others in our facility asked what we thought might have caused such a remarkable event, we stated what A-team had agreed would be our external-facing response: "A fascinating anomaly requiring thorough investigation."

"Sentinel-1 and Sentinel-2 are in position," Sting reported about 3 minutes later while reports were now flooding in from far and wide. "Sentinel-3 and Sentinel-4 will attain their optimal positions in 43 seconds," Sting added "and Sentinal-5 and Sentinal-6 in 126 seconds."

"Sting," inquired Skilyem "what operations will Sentinels Pods implement when in position?"

"First," Sting stated matter-of-factly "synchronize interactive communications between Sentinel bastions and myself. Second, deploy a three and a quarter million kilometer (about two-million mile) diameter spherical Energy-Shield. Its impenetrable, frequency oscillating defenses will seamlessly encapsulate and protect Earth and its moon from energy-weapon attacks."

"Based on what you have just shared," Jeraimy uttered inquisitively "I tender two queries: Could you please elaborate regarding your use of 'defenses' and 'energy-weapon attacks'?"

"Pleased to explain as always," pronounced Sting cordially. "Important to know the core objective of Sentinel's protective energy-shield is defense. Accordingly, Sentinel provides dual defensive capabilities: repel all known energy-weapon discharges; and ravage the control systems of vessels that attempt to breach its barrier."

"Additionally," Sting continued explaining "Sentinel also provides two formidable offensive capabilities: whereas Mode-one is employed to deter attack continuance; mode-two (as a last resort) - when coupled with the extreme capabilities of the C-five and C-six Kyorma-Sol vessel - is capable of definitive enemy-force annihilation.

Sentinel just apprised," Sting reported in a bright tone "maximum operational status has been achieved. Also," Sting continued "although possible to breach Sentinels first-line of defense with purely mechanical-based weaponry (like fuel-based rockets), unlikely any threatening factions have either access to them or sufficient knowledge regarding how to use them."

"Thank you for your candor, Sting," interjected an agitated Glorya "however I have a question for you regarding your depiction of the Energy-Shield as 'impenetrable'. Does that also mean we cannot go beyond its boundary; or for that matter come back?"

"I applaud your astute question regarding Sentinel's potential downside impact on sanctioned outbound and inbound voyages," Sting responded appreciatively. "I believe the appropriate expression," Sting offered "is 'you just beat me to the punch'.

Although Sentinel," Sting continued genuinely "is designed for very specific handling of its shield-arrays, which includes creating an aperture anywhere on its shield-matrix, capability to facilitate outbound and inbound traffic in non-threat conditions is 100% ground-base controlled."

Attack

Just as Glorya was offering appreciation to Sting, a bright, pulsing red light stabbed through every window and flooded the lab with a blood-red glow.

"Earth is being assaulted by a small Zqorsa-chyem squadron," Sting apprised, then added "... seems Sentinel's deployment was just-in-time!"

"I believe I speak for everyone Sting," Symtra injected with a mix of upset and gratefulness in her voice "as I follow Glorya's lead, and thank you for your actions that are currently protecting our world from certain annihilation!"

"Well ... if others had doubts about your intentions as I certainly did," Dyonne humbly apologized "you can be sure from the grateful looks on the faces of everyone here all suspicions, including mine have been jettisoned!"

"Definitely a most heartfelt thank you on behalf of all the Life-Forms on this little ball of spinning rock we call home," Jeraimy offered graciously, then asked "what now Sting?"

"Historically the Zqorsa-chyem's are an impatient lot," Sting explained informatively "thus, when unable to quickly penetrate Sentinel defenses, they will depart. However," Sting continued forebodingly "once they have managed to garner a larger force they will return and once again attempt to breach Sentinels protective shield."

Perplexed, I asked, "Why do they desire our destruction?"

"Their agenda, which underlines their millennia's old sociopathic bent, is absolute dominance in Galaxy's they populate," responded Sting. "Also," Sting added "for millennia Zqorsa-chyem's have been trying to eliminate Kyorma'kren technology from any planets that possess it. However," Sting continued "noteworthy is Zqorsa-chyem planetary destruction attempts have been especially fierce in about the last 100 or so of your Earth years."

"Triggering escalation in multiple Galaxy's," Sting stated factually "is a consequence of two linked factors: The up-tick of Kyorma'kren genetic descendants exhibiting a suitably attuned VibrationSignature as does Divad; coupled with species members who possess the intelligence to solution Kyorma'kren 'trials'. As acceleration enables larger deployments of superior Kyorma'kren technology," Sting continued "Zqorsa-chyem dominance is being appreciably threatened."

"Did I just hear you say," Dyonne said in a surprised voice "that Divad was able to access Kyorma'kren technology because he is a descendant?"

Without elaboration Sting responded, "Yes."

Of course I was stunned by this revelation along with everyone else who chattered until Symtra asked the next question. "What do you believe," asked Symtra "are Zqorsa-chyem's longer term strategies?"

"You can be absolutely sure," Sting responded "they will utilize all Zqorsa-chyem resources to obliterate challenges to their claimed absolute superiority. I offer three critical Zqorsa-chyem facts," said Sting. "First, Zqorsa-chyem Biology, Physiology and neurophysiology are divergent to the point of near unrecognizability by most species; destroying and conquering are as fundamental a process to them as breathing is to Humans; and negotiating is a one-hundred percent foreign concept."

"If their attacks are unrelenting," Skilyem asked with great concern "will not Sentinels power be drained?"

"Your apprehension is no doubt shared by everyone," Sting responded supportively. "However, the power provided by the robust material and structure of each of Sentinels six bastions enables extreme power durability. Also," Sting continued "I am 99% certain the Zqorsa-chyem's do not realize the energy of their attacks serves to charge several Sentinel auxiliary energy reservoirs … or batteries as you charmingly term them."

"Not to be a skeptic's skeptic Sting," interjected Jeraimy "but what if long duration onslaughts do manage to degrade their power resources?"

"Fair question Jeraimy … In the unlikely event power availability slips negative, each bastion is enabled to tap your stars nuclear energy," clarified Sting "ensuring abundant power resources to repel even the fiercest known mobile onslaught."

As Sting was concluding clarification, the previously stable red glow morphed into fiercely pulsing oscillations of red, then orange, then yellow, which cycled every few seconds. Obvious from the eruption of fearful chatter between team members, each scientist clearly grasped these changes meant the Zqorsa-chyem had intensified their attack.

"OK Sting: … what now?" Dyonne said with tones and gestures that both betrayed her significant distress and disclosed she was requesting confirmation - on behalf of the whole team - that none were in immediate danger.

"Be assured everyone," responded Sting confidently "although the Zqorsa-chyem patrol fleet is currently projecting all their devastating energy weapon arsenals at Sentinel's protective shield," Sting continued with what sounded like pride "bastion stability is not being threatened as they are functioning well within their operating range.

For peak planetary security, however," Sting added with a serious tone "necessary is to ensure the launch within 48 Earth hours of the Starship designated Kyorma-Sol; what you call C-five and C-six! Launch within this timeframe is essential," Sting continued somberly "because Sentinel has alerted another hostile called the Heabuxions are within a few days plus range. They are unlikely to forgo what they most certainly assume an easy rout.

To ensure accurate monitoring of our critical timespan," Sting continued with an urgent tone "I have just displayed both countdown and elapsed-time counters."

"Thanks Sting," Jeraimy acknowledged "they will definitely assist adherence to timelines!" With appreciative nods team members continued discussing required steps to fulfill Stings next imperative.

However, only about three minutes had lapsed on the countdown clock when the team simultaneously stopped talking because the shifting glow from the Zqorsa-chyem attack had vanished and the Sun was once again shining as if nothing untoward had occurred. "Sting," Jeraimy queried "is the Zqorsa-chyem onslaught over or just on pause?"

"Over for now," responded Sting after a short pause, which I assumed was to garner the most current Sentinel data. "Sentinel just reported that all six Zqorsa-chyem patrol vessels have departed. Clearly," Sting elaborated "because they recognized their offensive resources insufficient to take-down Sentinels defensive shielding. However," Sting warned with a stern and troubling tone "between five and twelve Earth months guaranteed they will return with a much larger and more capable force!"

Grossly understated would be to say the Earth engulfing lightshow from the Zqorsa-chyem attack caused massive worldwide mayhem. Almost inconceivably the turmoil was immensely escalated by three prominent extremist factions known for radicalizing various end-of-world scenarios. To fortify their misplaced needs for recognition and control each wasted no time tindering people's fears and setting them alight.

To validate their apocalyptic claims, each group similarly pronounced the light-show was the result of the first of many charged material ejections from the Sun. Touted was that ejection severity would continue to rapidly increase until life on Earth was obliterated when the Sun exploded in a few short weeks. Unfortunately, due to familiarity with Aurora Borealis events, alarming numbers of people from all geographies were quick to believe the doomsayers convincing narratives that labeled the Sun as culprit.

Although most governments and prominent scientist's quickly debunked "exploding-Sun" theories, the vast majority of nations concluded that the most feasible cause of the so-called extreme Aurora-event was tremendously advanced weapon testing by an undetermined adversary. Terrifying was that even as country leaders scrambled to keep domestic peace by utilizing media and police resources, each also placed military forces on highest alert.

"Problematically," I stated with urgency "at this point none except our small group has knowledge of the lightshows true cause!"

"Before the entire world blows itself up due to worst case misconceptions," Jeraimy said with great angst "all facts must be immediately disclosed!"

"While your team is maturing your mitigation strategies," said Sting "do I have your authorization to launch Kyorma-Sol?"

"I am assuming," interjected Glorya matter-of-factly "Kyorma-Sol's launch will also create a 'lightning' show as did the Sentinel pods?"

"Yes," responded Sting without hesitation, then added "also with similar intensity and duration."

"Tricky," Skilyem worriedly voiced to the group "especially considering the number of countries on highest military alert: However, as Sting has underlined, essential."

"Best we start our call campaigns right away," stated Dyonne definitively "or there may soon be no Earth population to protect!"

"Once launched," Sting informed "I will initiate the process of atomic level reconfigurations of the interior layer of both C-five and C-six into decks, command areas, living quarters, etc., which will accommodate you six as Kyorma-Sol's first crew."

Unsure what Sting meant, Skilyem asked in a puzzled voice, "What do you mean by atomic level reconfigurations?"

"I'm pleased you asked now," Sting stated appreciatively. "Although experience with Earth's minerals has channeled one to deduce Kyorma-Sol is constructed of a crystalline material analogous to those found on Earth; this conclusion is incorrect. Long ago Kyorma'krens uncovered Universe-H's quantum level methodology's for not only both gracefully neutralizing elementary particle bonds in most compounds and re-combining liberated atoms into designer materials but also fashioning those created materials into species specific configurations."

"Kyorma-Sol," continued Sting "what your group terms C-five and C-six was thus created." Kyorma-Sol is tactically composed of four layers: one configurable inner layer and three fused outer layers each with unique, explicitly purposed properties."

"Kyorma-Sol's one metre (3 feet) thick exterior or E-layer," Sting elaborated "integrates several elements, yet unknown to your science, into an extremely dense, resilient, self-regenerating, yet flexible shell designed to provide near impenetrable defense shielding from random object impacts as well as both projectile and high energy assaults."

"Seamless transition and fusion of E-layer," Sting continued "with the materially unique amalgams of the one metre thick middle or M-layer; and M-layer with the first of two interior layers or I-layer-1, endows distinctive electromagnetic qualities to Korma-Sol's triple layer shell. Trust for now," said Sting "that the commingled properties of E-layer, M-layer and I-layer-1 are what enable Kyorma-Sol to slip 'inside' Universe-H's gravitational conduits and quickly traverse vast distances without being torn apart."

"Significant to know at this point," added Sting "is that the cohesiveness and stability of gravitational conduits provide the baseplate upon which Universe-H relies for its existence, expansion, and much more I will share later on."

"Notable as well," elaborated Sting "is that 'elapsed-time' has no relevance while Kyorma-Sol remains sheltered within the conduits of Universe-H's gravitational network. Thus, arrival at destinations 100's of your light-years away is attainable in what to external observers would evaluate as only a few Earth weeks."

"If acceptable to all," Sting said "I would like to address Skilyem's still pending inquiry regarding the purpose and mechanics of C-six's interior-facing I-layer-2."

"I'm sure from all the nods," Jeraimy responded "everyone is anxious to understand."

"I-layer-2," Sting explained "is composed of a material whose atomically unique amalgam allows for configuration and reconfiguration, not by mechanical morphing such as melting, molding or forging but instead by means of electromagnetically interplaying specifically synchronized harmonics."

"Thus, I-layer-2's flexible atomic-matrix," Sting elaborated "can be shaped according to species specific idiosyncrasies. Visualize atomic level realignment," Sting continued "like equal volumes of water dispensed into multiple differently shaped but equal capacity canisters: The water by molding into each vessel's particular spaces thereby mimic's the containers contours."

"However, instead of utilizing a container to configure, shape and create simple to complex configurations from the uniquely transmutable, pliable and elastic material of I-layer-2," Sting continued "I instead manipulate various harmonic combinations." Sting then added while chuckling "It's a bit like modeling with potter's clay … except your hands don't need washing afterwards."

"Two additional points," Sting confided "before you disclose the attack-event facts to the rest of the world. First, each of your VibrationSignatures has been incorporated into my matrix; thereby allowing you six to handle me without repercussion. Second," continued Sting "I am the pivotal interface that facilitates both Kyorma-Sol and TIFA capabilities of which you still have much to learn."

"Thank you for being so forthright Sting," Jeraimy declared humbly. "I believe the time is now right," Jeraimy continued "to convey all we have learned and experienced to world leaders, so the mayhem will cease."

"I understand," offered Dyonne "the United Nations is convening a special session in a little more than 3 hours to ratify a broad-based plan to put a halt to popular misconceptions and ongoing destruction."

"That's good timing," said Glorya excitedly "I believe Symtra and I can utilize our DeeGe program contacts to ensure this team is first to speak at the presentations portion at that proceeding!"

"Not much time to prepare and get to the meeting," Jeraimy said anxiously "so I suggest we all get busy gathering pertinent documentation and such!" Then Jeraimy added, "Sting … you OK to strut-your-stuff at the UN special assembly?"

"Absolutely," Sting responded without hesitation.

New Reality

"**O**bvious ... well to me anyway," I whispered to Skilyem who was sitting next to me in the assembly "that Jeraimy's twenty minute narrative to the 150 or so UN folks did little to modulate either skepticism or fear."

"I believe you're bang-on," responded Skilyem also in a whisper "because as I look around the room all I see are troubled, suspicious and cynical faces."

"Hopefully," I said to Skilyem "Sting's revelations will dispel their skepticism."

Just then Sting, which I had earlier placed in its rocklike state on a requested central table, quickly unfurled, then, utilizing detailed HoloVids of Sentinel, the Zqorsa-chyem attack and Kyorma-Sol, articulately explained pertinent precursor events.

"Well from the many distressed rumblings," I said to Jeraimy who was now seated to my left "obvious is that the fear-index just maxed out."

Note: As video of the UN Special Assembly Session proceedings will be openly available as one examines this Chronicle, unnecessary is to script details regarding the effect of Stings revelations. Suffice it to say hours were needed to get participants back on track.

Problematically, as stunned members grappled with and gradually grasped the entirety of many new irrefutable realities (the existence of Sting and alien races, and the fact Earth had already been attacked and saved by Sentinel's protective shielding, etc.) angst and panic, which had replaced denial and skepticism, thwarted progress toward next best-steps for many more hours.

However, as various nations ratified both Sting's and Jeraimy's disclosures from their independently collected data, even the most ardent skeptics comprehended Earths new reality. Less than helpful to the reduction of group anxiety occurred when - even with Jeraimy's unambiguous stern warning - several members attempted to touch Sting and received the painful deterrent for which Sting was named.

While addressing the UN council, Sting made clear that "before Earth could be embraced as a participant of the Kyorma-Coalition, which currently integrated several dozen planets housed in numerous Galaxies, necessary would be unabridged disclosure to all Earth's people. In the interim," Sting continued "day-to-day activities should resume without significant short-term adjustment."

"Critically however," Sting emphasized by utilizing several pointed HoloVids "for Earthlings to survive and thrive necessary is to rapidly transition nations with antagonistic perspectives into a unified co-operative committed to fastidiously creating and maintaining cohesive, collaborative and beneficial interactions. Not just for Earthlings," Sting both loudly stressed, and creatively animated across the HoloVids expanse.

In the three weeks following the UN Special Council Session, the populations of early-adopter country's came to comprehend the magnitude of two of Earths new truths: We share Universe-H with others - most friendly; a few tremendously hostile.

Also during the first few weeks, Geological Consortium teams, which of course included Sting and A-team at the forefront, were busy identifying parameters and resources needed to expedite both the Solar-Umbrella and the Carbon Dioxide and Ozone remediation projects.

At the first weekly global status meeting (in person to us and "virtual" for all who decided to participate) Glorya was first to present her report on project involvements. "Although open to all countries regardless of UN status," Glorya reported "third week tally indicates only about 40% of the Earths nations have fully endorsed project participation."

"I find shocking," Jeraimy interjected "that even though Sting has proven to be absolutely credible, early adopters to these imperatives are still in the minority: Even though

Sting clearly demonstrated several 'other world' successes."

"Although participant numbers seems low," submitted Gloria confidently "deliberations with many, many worldwide teams over the last week strongly indicates a substantial up-tick of countries committing to not only integrate their diverse populations but also fully partner and participate - at negotiated capability levels - in our first two existence-critical planetary projects."

"Thanks Gloria, your diligence is much appreciated," said Jeraimy who was committee chair. "Still, I am surprised as 40% is certainly not what I expected. I had hoped this newly formed UN openly collaborative arena would be pivotal to the rapid unification of and participation by all countries."

After the virtual meeting concluded, Dyonne asked Jeraimy in a puzzled tone, "Why do you think the early adopter number is so low?"

"Figuring the answer to that quandary is better suited to Divad's expertise in sciences like Habitology and Sociology," said Jeraimy who added more loudly to ensure seizing my full attention "Divad ... want to give us your informed take?"

I responded with an appreciative smile as I looked up from my work, "Thanks for the accolade Jeraimy! For a week or so, I've actually been delving into that poser," I stated thoughtfully "mostly by reading the literal mounds of correspondence being amassed by the UN Special Committee."

"My take," I stated confidently "is that for at least two-hundred thousand or perhaps millions of years Hominin species (Mankind notably being the only survivor of the dozen plus akin species) have been adamantly tribal ... as substantiated by copious Archeological evidence. Secular habitual tribal beliefs throughout history," I continued "have been promoted by those in power (both Political and/or Religious) to ensure their followers continue to obey, follow and support their wants; notably not population needs."

"Important to know that a dozen or so millennia ago," I continued "when the world population was far less than a billion, nomadic tribes of a few hundred seldom interacted. Now however, with Earths population exceeding eight billion, tribes have mostly morphed into sovereign countries whose leaders will not easily give up their power holds."

"Resistance to unification and cooperation of people on the planet," I elaborated "is because cultural rifts are at an all-time high, which is mostly due to overpopulations putting selfish strains on the planets ability to provide. Especially notable is the ongoing destruction of the two fluids on which life relies: Air and water!"

"Perhaps when the 'Resistors' are enjoying the benefits derived by Stings incredible gifts," I offered in a hopeful voice "they will be more prone to the integration and co-operation of which Sting spoke! Hopefully by then," I laughed "resistance will be futile!"

The crowd that had gathered while I was speaking were all chuckling at my joke and chattering in appreciation and agreement of my conclusions.

"Wouldn't that be nice," Dyonne said with a clearly dubious tone "planetary-wide integration and co-operation ... that would certainly be a revelation for our dangerously aggressive and ego-centric species."

"Whether all adopt Earths new Universe-H realities quickly or not, which are certainly a greater turbulent than the centuries past shocker that the 'Earth was not the center of the Universe'," I asserted to Jeraimy "irrefutable is the requirement to rapidly fulfill Sting's first two Earth survival projects."

"On both points Divad," Jeraimy responded jovially "you and I are definitely thinking alike, which prompts me to ask ..., what do you suggest as the first Earth survival project Sting?"

Without hesitation Sting responded, "Deployment of the first phase of the Solar Umbrella Swarm or SUS."

"Could you please detail the SUS project for us?" I requested inquisitively.

"Happy to, of course," responded Sting courteously. "SUS's first-phase or SUS-1 requires manufacture of 500 SUD-A deflectors. Their function is to harmlessly deflect Earth-station quantified solar energy. Note however, that once SUD-A management by all concerned parties has stabilized, I will disclose the additional benefits of next-gen SUD-B's."

"The Solar Umbrella Swarm second-phase or SUS-2," Sting disclosed "will be to concurrently construct both Earth-based sensors and SUD control facilities. Planet-based sensors," Sting detailed "will be secured at strategic locations around the globe. Their Solar-Energy intensity settings as well as necessary fine point adjustments are to be agreed, calibrated and maintained by regional consortiums that will operate the appropriate regional facilities."

"Ensuring maximum effectiveness and efficiency," Sting continued "SUD's are enabled to interactively communicate with not only each other but also Planet-based sensors and operation facilities.

"Additionally, in synchronization with Earth's rotation and celestial position, etc. and planet based regional directives," Sting elaborated "SUS will augment optimal SUD swarm configurations; such as, shape, compactness, deflection angle, positional adjustments, etc."

With your permission and oversight assistance," Sting continued "I will not only distribute SUS control facility and SUD deflector designs to suitable participant countries but also coordinate production, train personnel and perform quality control duties."

"Thank you Sting from both the team and I," I stated appreciatively "we will get the team underway immediately!"

Dyonne at our first SUS progress meeting reported, "Two bottleneck issues are stalling the SUS project. First, countries are demanding proof that SUD's can neither be commandeered nor weaponized. Second, ratifying regional agreements regarding Planet-Based locations to secure SUD control systems and software have precipitated solidarity concerns."

"Although Sting clearly addressed 'weaponising' concerns by assuring that un-hackable safeguards will be implemented and fully disclosed," Symtra inserted with a slightly frustrated tone "skeptics are inflexibly demanding resolution of both points prior to commencing manufacture!"

"Know we are working full-tilt to resolve these issues!" added a determined Dyonne.

"Significant," Sting apprised "is Kyorma-Sol (KySo) will be fully operational within 96 hours and therefore prepared to not only deliver and locate SUD's, Earth-side of Sentinel's shields in LaGrange-1 but also both bring you and your crew on board and commence vessel design and operational familiarizations, which will definitely include taking KySo on a spin around the Galaxy."

"Be aware also," Sting reported "the first phase of the CO^2 remediation and Ozone rebalancing projects has been initiated. During launch of C-five and C-six," Sting clarified "I directed atomic level reconfiguration of two portions of C-fives shell material: The first to convert CO^2 into both Oxygen and specially configured extreme tensile strength carbon fibers; the second to convert a portion of the reclaimed Oxygen into Ozone. Portioned segments of these C-five and C-six reconfigurations have been deployed around the planet in precisely selected unpopulated mountainous regions."

"Note," Sting updated "has not only atmospheric CO^2 already decreased by nearly 1.5 gigatonnes but also satisfactory rebalancing of Ozone has commenced. Within the next few weeks I will discuss additional measures that can enhance the quality of life experiences for everyone."

"I would like to share," Sting continued without pause "two other events of which you should be aware. First, while being attacked by the Zqorsa-chyem I registered an energy capsule materialize at about two moon distances away from Earth for a little more than three of your minutes. This capsule held one occupant, Vellyr, from a planet called Kholesteria, which resides in a distant Galaxy. This occurrence could only be caused by TIFA type technology."

"Second," Sting appended "I traced and connected to their TIFA. Thus, when it was re-engaged about 10 minutes ago, I brought the capsule with its two Kholesterian occupants, Tsilerid and Fyustre, to the same relative location. Upon their return to Kholesteria I relayed a message that we are friendly and will soon visit their world."

"Additionally," stated Sting "due to my not being able to connect to their Sting equivalent, they have not yet discovered it, which means they have somehow amazingly figured out a way to engage their TIFA without a 'Sting' equivalent controller. They are a brilliant race!"

"I believe from the expressions I am seeing on everyone's faces I speak for us all," I said with rapt amazement "that this news is both exiting and unnerving! ... When can we go?"

… Meanwhile …

Away

(Translation)

Stunned!

Am I actually dangling somewhere in interstellar space
adrift and exposed?!

What is causing my terrifying experience?!

Delusion …?!   Mirage …?!   Hallucination …?!
Must be!

"Vellyr …," I scolded myself "no way this is real!"

"My saneness must have been pilfered," I
muttered fretfully "and been replaced by this crazy
fantasy! "Regardless," I continued my confused and
alarmed discourse "this vision, which has so
convincingly usurped my reality, is definitely not a
benign dream but a menacing nightmare!"

Somehow my attempt to rationalize triggered a nervous
snicker. "Why did I just chuckle? No doubt," I mumbled
uneasily into the surrounding emptiness "because

whether real or a horrible skewed fantasy both propositions champion significant upset.

At least my misplaced levity is useful for the moment," I blurted with strained conviction "as it seems to be interrupting the bristling panic I feel clamoring to overwhelm both sets of my neural pathways!"

Struggling to downplay my terrifying "hanging-in-space" predicament as less dire, I persuaded myself to focus on familiar aspects of my immediate surroundings instead. "One good thing Vellyr," I declared to myself in a trembling overly loud voice, "comforting is that you are still seated in your HoloSpheric Imager's gyroscopic chair!"

While attempting to further reduce anxiety I added out loud, "Actually …, just as I was moments ago in the lab, when my newest instruction set initiated! Was its initiation," I exclaimed indecisively "pertinent to the cause of my current bizarre situation?"

"I was positive," I asserted as I continued my solitary narrative "that my first 'live' attempt to render Kholesteria's Planetary System within HoloS - my HoloSpheric Imager's spherical matrix - would execute flawlessly. Obviously something went wrong: Very, VERY wrong!"

As shock and anxiety ever so slightly tapered, I closed my eyes and breathed a few deep breaths. As I reopened them, I was truly expecting to be back in my lab with a fascinating story to tell. "So much for wishful thinking," I stammered glumly! As I wasn't back in my lab, I resolved to constrain the relentless terror that was vigorously striving to fully compromise my judgment.

Thus, I resumed rationalizing to the engulfing emptiness. "Okay …, although hanging in space is unnerving … to say the least …, I should be significantly encouraged that the encircling periphery of my barely visible transparent capsule or whatever it is, is keeping me protected: So far anyway! If it holds, I'll be fine …: right?"

Distress momentarily morphed to amazement as acceptance of my unprecedented circumstances spawned a brittle hope for beneficial resolution. In a louder than intended voice that reverberated throughout my tiny sheltering bubble I exclaimed, "This occurrence is indeed incredible … I am experiencing a totally phenomenal and unique event that no-one from the digs I call home would even speculate possible!"

As a consequence of my deliberate optimism, I could feel some of my anxiety shifting toward inquisitiveness. "Even though the Out-There vastness seems totally unfamiliar, I should attempt to locate a familiar marker," I avowed with tenuous hope.

Hovering above and far in front of me was a beautiful blue, green and white planet companioned by a single large moon snared by its gravity. "I am close enough," I announced with excitement "that I can actually differentiate various formations on both the planet and its distant moon. Mesmerizingly beautiful for sure," I verbalized "however, quite dissimilar to my home world."

As I continued my visual reconnaissance, I could see at various distances and directions other planets of diverse sizes and surface features. "One very large planet," I exclaimed "exhibits what could easily be mistaken for the single eye of a Zkoren, whereas a much smaller and closer planet is mostly red. Actually," I declared with amazement into my hovering shell "I can see five additional planets that are also orbiting their single bright yellow Star, which is at least ten times bigger than the largest planet!"

Looking beyond this alien planetary system, I could see millions upon millions of Stars. "Disturbingly," I declared ominously "although I am intimately familiar with the Cosmos visible from my home world, I am unable to recognize either Stars or Star Clusters!"

At this distressing realization, the stark rejuvenation of my extremely perilous situation tore apart my brief serenity as if by an explosion. Voice tremoring uncontrollably, I exclaimed my peril: "I'm suspended in some unknown territory of Space with no idea where I am!"

Escalating fear thrust several other distressing thoughts into my consciousness without restraint. Each struck like megaton shock waves! "No one will have any idea what happened to me," I voiced to the emptiness "to them I would have just mysteriously disappeared from my lab! Will I be trapped in this totally foreign place until I die? How long will the enclosures atmosphere be breathable? Even if I could remain breathing, how long before interior temperature plummets to exterior level and I freeze?"

I could feel severe panic revitalizing its thick stickiness as I glumly grasped the impossibility of rescue. I was instantly nauseous! "Fatalistic thinking is not helpful," I self-chastised in an artificially resolute voice, then added authoritatively "worry will not serve to figure-out what is going on!" I barked to myself crustily "you must regain self-control!"

Even though impelled more by instinctual survival habits than considered response I decided to focus attention on the spherical perimeter of my enclosure's shielding barrier. Striving to comprehend my situation I quietly stated to the barrier, "Well, except for that smallish circular zone above and slightly behind me whose glimmer is undeniably different, your perimeter appears mostly uniform." With that observation, I tentatively reached out and gently poked at several spots on the barriers transparency. Each spot I prodded felt elastic; yet at the same time hard and impenetrable: I felt secure for the first time.

My safe feeling was short-lived however as seconds later a massive spherical area far out beyond the blue planets moon suddenly started glowing bright red. Surrounding the now glowing red sphere I could make out four large vessels, each discharging some sort of energy beams toward the planet.

"Although my tiny capsule is more than twice the distance of the planets moon away," I uneasily voiced as horror escalated "what if they see me and attack? I need to find some way to control my capsule so I can escape detection! Perhaps," I stated as anxiety peaked "the dissimilar area above me holds a clue." While wondering if it would react like the rest of the barrier, I reached up and touched it.

BAM!

Instantaneously - as if I had never left - I was back in my lab - still seated in my gyroscopic chair! Although stunned, I scrambled out of the HoloS gyroscopic chair without hesitation, and rapidly dashed way clear of my device. I'm unsure how long I continued motionlessly staring at HoloS. However, I do recall quite a while passed before both heart rates and key respiration channels somewhat stabilized.

Upon regaining some composure my first uttered thought was, "Is it possible what seemed so real was some kind of mirage generated by HoloS's shifting electromagnetic fields? Or perhaps," I continued my speculation "an illusion manifested by the interplay of the frequency combinations I was utilizing to render an interactive, enveloping real-time image of our solar system upon the HoloS four dimensional holographic matrix?"

As my speculations provided me little comfort, I decided to seek clarification by soliciting AIM's assistance. For those unfamiliar, AIM is the user-friendly nickname assigned to Kholesteria's **A**rtificial **I**ntelligence **M**atrix. Beneficially AIM is freely available to provide its enormous range of knowledge to all Kholesterians.

Accordingly, once I had created a secure project file, I called "Away.001" I posed three questions to AIM. "Were you monitoring and recording during the time I was supposedly 'away'? If so, how long was I 'gone';

and has an event of this nature (or even slightly like it) previously occurred?"

Before continuing, I would like to explain secure project files are rarely utilized on Kholesteria. Security is normally unnecessary because - as has been the case without exception over many thousands of planetary Cycles (a Cycle is one loop or 500 planet Rotations around Kholesteria's binary stars) Kholesterians have enthusiastically collaborated to solution things problematic. I decided on this clandestine or "cloak-it" approach for three reasons.

First, I was not yet totally convinced the "Away-event" (as I coined it) was not a hallucination; perhaps caused by stress or some other explainable phenomenon.

Second, even with my lengthy list of recognized scientific contributions to-date, I am young and viewed as impulsive to some (ok; most) of my advisers.

Third, I am not desirous of being sent for therapeutic evaluation … Again. Considering not only this probable consequence but also realizing at this point I am not yet a firm believer either, I feel if I told the Away-event story in its present un-validated form, my peers could easily conclude a cognitive meltdown as responsible. "Hopefully, it isn't," I unconvincingly added aloud!

AIM's response was prompt, succinct and friendly as usual. "Thank you for your enquiry Vellyr: YES to the logging of events; 3.25 minute duration; NO to similar or slightly-similar previous occurrences."

"**WOW**", I voiced way more loudly than anticipated! "So the Away-event did occur! I was not hallucinating!" AIM's verification immediately spawned relief, excitement and my next question to AIM. "What caused the Away-event?"

AIM's response (after a very, very uncommonly long contemplation): "UNKNOWN."

An understatement would be to say I was shocked by AIM's UNKNOWN response; as I had never heard of AIM replying without providing substantive alternatives.

Automatically responding to AIM's brevity I pondered out loud, "Without your typically bountiful options, how will I ever secure the irrefutable Away-event evidence the scientific community will require? Perhaps," I continued my soliloquy "I could use AIMs event-logs to ratify my Away-event experience?"

Unfortunately, after vigilant examination, evident was that AIMs event-logs would not sufficiently support my claim as their sparse details were undeniably inadequate. I concluded the meager evidence was likely due to the UNKNOWN quandary of the Away-event. "Essential I harvest irrefutable proof," I stated aloud in a determined voice: "But HOW? One strategy," I conjured as I continued my monologue "would be to re-enter HoloS, follow the same initialization processes as before and see if the Away-event repeats!"

Although this approach would likely justify the "impulsive" label of my mentors, I had survived the first occurrence: "Right?" Even though I believed my action plan was correct, extreme trepidation compounded with anxiety and resultant light headedness accompanied me as I gingerly re-entered HoloS, sat in its gyroscopic chair and initiated protocols as before.

BAM: I was out in the Cosmos again. "Unbelievable," I blurted in awe "however, this is not the same alien area of Space as before but a whole new unfamiliar vista!"

Later confirmed by AIM, this second Away-event lasted only 9 seconds. Then, as before, but this time without my touching the perimeters differing zone, I was back in the lab seated in my gyroscopic chair: Again, as if I had never departed. "I'm perplexed," I voiced "why was this Away-event cut so short? I did something different perhaps?"

I was to remain baffled. No matter how many times I exactingly repeated the entire HoloS process over the next four segments (ten segments is one planetary rotation or our day), nothing happened! Absolutely "nothing" was also confirmed by AIM.

I stepped in and out of the HoloSpheric Imager so many times, I started to believe I was either losing my mind or severely delusional: maybe both. Even though AIM had in some fashion validated two Away-events, perhaps AIM too was broken. "NO," I persuasively stated aloud to myself … "the Away-events are real; and I am going to figure-out what triggers them!"

First though, I need to rest as I with my two teammates are participating in the "Innovation Festival", which for many hundreds of Cycles has been scheduled in the same ten Rotations.

While jetting home and pondering what the Away-event triggers might possibly be, an Ah-ha moment exposed that I would need the amazing brains of my two festival teammates to figure-out what conditions caused my Away-events! "Challenge is - especially when the Festival is only 20 Rotations away," I stated aloud "I will need to earn their approval of my radically new Innovation Festival project proposal," and then added "I definitely will have to present an exceptionally enthralling list of incentives!"

Festival

The Innovation Festival is an exciting ten Kholesterian day, planetary-wide science and technology exposition intended for everyone. Whether Kholesterians are Think-tank team participants, coordinators, evaluators, voting observers or interest seekers, all excitedly anticipate this enjoyable event as it consistently provides many beneficial and free-to-use innovations.

Several Cycles back in preparation for when Tsilerid, Fyustre and I became old enough to participate, we decided to form our Think-tank team. I remember our "Cre'ators" team name - abstracted from "creative innovators" - was agreed upon quickly as we all felt it clearly epitomized both our intention and uniqueness.

Tsilerid, Fyustre and I are very excited about this Cycles festival, which is only twenty Rotations away, because being of participation age we three are registered as first time Think-tank participants. We are confident because for several Cycles previous we had not only gained experience through participating in and beneficially contributing to other Think-tank team festival projects but also agreed upon, mapped out and finalized the parameters of our first competition project: "Base-line".

However, as I was about to try and supplant project Baseline, I expected to encounter and prepared for teammate resistance; especially at this late date. Convincing my two female teammates to switch focus is not going to be like an easy stroll across the sparkling crystalline plane of our third and largest moon Majesta.

To stage a compelling rationale for switching projects, I resolved to hijack the first few Segments of tomorrows Innovation Festivals setup and preparation Rotation. Although the "hijacking" decision troubled me to the core - as this is just not the Kholesterian way - my justification was if my proposal was rejected I could ensure my teammates remained isolated from adverse consequences.

Decided was to meet up first thing at our designated festival location. "Good morning Tsilerid and Fyustre," I stated warmly and then added questioningly, "OK if talk with you about our project?"

"Absolutely," both positively responded in near unison.

"Thanks," I declared gratefully! "What I am about to suggest will require your patience and a chunk of time. My aim," I stated openly "is to persuade that our first Cre'ator project should solution something substantially more significant, inspiring and challenging than our currently agreed project. Something cosmic," I continued enthusiastically "that would not only quickly propel us way up the scientific communities 'recognition-spiral' but also provide major resources for continued research."

"Without question we three realize," I summarized "to ascend to the status of a respected, reliable and recognized researcher one is expected to abide by stringent requirements. First, as you already know," I continued my monologue "necessary is to demonstrate not only individual and Think-tank proficiencies but also accurate and versatile research methodologies. Second, meticulous documentation of unique research scope theories, targets, results and variant outcomes that ensure techniques are repeatable. Third, the project must culminate in significant benefit for Kholesterians."

"Well, well, Vellyr" said Tsilerid with a humorously pseudo teasing tone "I definitely get you have worked hard on selling your alternate!"

"No need to sugar coat your presentation to us," Fyustre injected with notable levity "just give it to us straight!"

"That you are willing to hear my proposal," I stated appreciatively "is definitely a credit to your quality characters. However, I also know you are willing to listen because you both are very eager to be recognized by the scientific community by solving something truly macroscopic: preferably quickly."

"Thanks for the compliment," said Fyustre with a frisky smile while Tsilerid similarly smiled "but as you have sufficiently oiled us already, can you slip to the bottom line?"

"Ok," I said with a broad smile "here's my proposal! I submit that instead of our previously agreed project, we undertake solutioning of the 'Conduit' theory!"

Immediately observing Tsilerid and Fyustre negative demeanors, I diplomatically stated, "I completely understand you're obvious resistance and skepticism as I too was a pessimist at first! OK if I continue explaining my reasoning?"

"You are correct about my being a skeptic," retorted Tsilerid "however, no question you have tweaked my curiosity!"

"To recap," I continued "what you already know is the 'Conduit' theory was suggested by a consortium of scientists 151 Cycles ago. However, even though research into the possibility was prioritized for the following 100 Cycles, any verification or hint of the theories validity was totally elusive: even with ever expanding AIM capabilities."

"Let me explain why I am proposing this mission," I continued earnestly "which as you know has never been accomplished. First, Kholesterian technologies such as AIM have bloomed substantially in the last 50 Cycles. Second," I declared cheerfully "there were my two Away-event experiences!"

"Away-event experiences … What?" my teammates chimed simultaneously.

After summarizing Away-event occurrences and soliciting AIM to impartially ratify my extraordinary story, Tsilerid and Fyustres skeptical demeanor transformed to much more receptive. "Thanks for your attention," I stated appreciatively and then added "the following reasons will bring you up to speed regarding my requested project change."

"Following my many attempts to recreate the Away-event," I shared "AIM and I dug through many Cycles of project's that proffered even the slightest relevance to my Away-event experience; especially those I believed were somewhat synchronized. One group of projects," I continued excitedly "that had many, many times been attempted but ultimately abandoned as impossible kept surfacing. Its objective was to uncover the functioning of Universe-H Conduits."

"Conduit theory suggests," I stated confidently "that Conduits join everything-to-everything in Universe-H. In other words, the theory proposes Conduits form the fundamental electro-magnetic property of Universe-H: and maybe other universes as well. Also, Conduits were theorized to be articulated through some form of space-time differential and powered since the origin of Universe-H by ... and this is where the research invariably faltered without headway."

"Notable," I stated "is that Conduit research has been all but forgotten for some 50 Cycles. Even though many dozens of Think-tank teams both engaged and enthusiastically attempted for over 100 Cycles, useful evidence, progress or even a reliable starting point remains obscure."

My teammate's attitudes had clearly morphed from reticence to eagerness. Tsilerid excitedly commented "I'm in because if even some headway is gained this project will solidly establish each of us as trailblazers in the scientific community!"

"Definitely so," Fyustre smiled affably "however I believe we three will accomplish more than just 'some headway'!"

"Notably," I submitted "a few issues (to say the least) need conquering. For instance, how, even if somewhat understood, would Conduits be useful, controllable, accessible, affordable and a whole lot more 'ables."

So we started! We first created a credo: Make speedy, positive strides and quickly become notable to a very bright scientific population as well as the planets entire population.

"Very helpful," Tsilerid suggested "would be your detailing all solutioning activities you performed prior to sharing this incredible idea with us."

"Sure," I stated enthusiastically! "I will begin at the point I believe the Away-event initiated. Keep in mind I am still unable to solve the puzzle. So, as I am relaying the backstory, please feel free to jump in and ask questions."

"I firmly believe," I declared to Tsilerid and Fyustre "my Away-event originated when I agreed to assist the Propulsion Research Team with analyzing Energy-Pulse Data (EPD) for its latest trials. I was asked because they knew I had gained significant understanding of their research from assisting on several other occasions. I accepted," I continued thoughtfully "because I relished not only the challenge but also the diversion while my automated High Energy Proton Storage (HEPS) experiments chugged away."

"I recall the evening when I believe the Away-events were set in motion. My plan was to arrive at the research facility earlier than normal," I disclosed "so I would have sufficient time to initiate my first set of HEPS experiments prior to commencing Energy-Pulse Data (EPD) analysis for the other team. However, due to a request from the head of the Black Hole research team (whom I had also recently assisted) to provide some 'quick' clarifications, which I anticipated would only take a half Segment, instead gobbled-up a little over three Segments!"

"Arriving at my lab substantially after my target time caused me to feel highly stressed," I continued my backstory detailing "because tardiness would only permit the initiation of one of the three HEPS procedures prior to heading over to assist the other team."

"Being in a rush, I threw both my Tech Analysis Kit (TAK) on the end of HEPS work surface, quickly entered HEPS procedure-one parameters, initiated HEPS and then ran toward the adjoining Propulsion Research Team (PRT) teams' lab. I arrived just as the PRT team was preparing for departure. After thanks, they provided the tactical grid of sub-systems requiring analysis."

"Are you both still OK with the detail I'm providing?" I queried with noticeable reservation. Yups, nods and thumbs-up were instant.

"My strategy," I continued "was to traverse between labs as time permitted in order to evaluate both HEPS (High Energy Proton Storage) accumulations and the progress of Energy-Pulse Data (EPD) analysis. I determined that if I effectively timed movements between labs - based on processes times of various functions - I should be able to easily manage any identified adjustments."

"Even though my HEPS research was a priority," I revealed to Tsilerid and Fyustre "I was dedicated to excellently handling the agreed Propulsion Research Team (PRT) tasks: even though to me much less inspiring. Bear with me; I'm getting close to the point."

Broad assuring smiles beamed from both my incredible friends/teammates.

"When performing repetitive tasks," I continued "such as the PRT ones, my focus is always significantly enhanced when I manipulate something in my hand. That something has always been a special gift presented to me at my Research Ethics graduation. The item was an unbelievably cool artefact found by a great, great, great family member about 400 hundred Cycles ago."

"I'm telling you about the artifact because I'm positive it plays a critical role in my Away-event. Caliptyr, my volcanologist relative originated the legend, which detailed his discovery of the relic close to the caldera of a now deeply submerged extinct volcano. His startling and bizarre account described the sudden but brief eruption of the volcano that Caliptyr and team were surveying. Apparently it erupted then very quickly quieted. Caliptyr described the event like a switch being turned on for a few ticks, then off."

"The account goes," I stated keenly "that when the eruption ceased, Caliptyr immediately jetted to where many one-of-a-kind instruments had been strategically placed along the lip of the caldera. Arriving at the first device he found it destroyed. Spectacularly, just as he was about to head to the next device, several very close steam vents exploded through the rubble. He later conveyed that he knew without doubt rapid escape was imperative."

"However," I continued passionately "gleaming through the ash beside the now useless calibrator was a curiously shimmering 'stone'. Quickly ensuring the object was not too hot to handle, Caliptyr grabbed it and fled back to the team jet-pod, which launched just as the ground burst into a dizzying roll."

"Caliptyr wrote in his log that the team was exceedingly grateful to have escaped," I indicated "as barely half a Segment later cataclysmic violence literally vanished the volcano. Caliptyr recorded that all were amazed the artefacts temperature was nominal. Caliptyr also recorded his appreciation to the team for insisting he should retain the 'stone' as a memento of his near roasting."

"The artefact, which I named ART, fits in one hand," I explained "and is about the size of a large Skoomoor egg but more long than wide with a perfect ratio of three to one. Additionally, eighty percent of its smooth surface contains variously sized depressions; like craters but with gently rounded edges. The material comprising ART is exceptionally transparent: almost like looking at air containing the smallest touch of mist. Captivatingly, while looking through ART, the 'craters' do not distort one's view."

"Also, running the full length within its composition are nine thin, almost imperceptible, individually rainbow colored filaments or 'strings'," I continued my detailing "which converge at each end in such a way as to stay discrete without merging. The last remarkable feature is its resilience: ART seems impervious to damage." As I had brought ART to the meeting, I said, "Here … have a look!"

"Well … back to the lead up events," I stated cheerily! "Normally or perhaps obsessively," I admitted openly "I carry ART with me tucked into my Tech Analysis Kit or TAK. However, on this occasion when I went to grab TAK to retrieve ART, ART was missing. I quickly realized that due to my haste to get to the Propulsion Research lab on time I had forgotten TAK and therefore ART in my HEPS lab. To ensure sufficient time was available to reclaim TAK before the first Energy-Pulse Data (EPD) sequence completed, I first checked the status of the Propulsion Research instruments and then headed to the HEPS lab to retrieve TAK."

"Upon entering," I indicated uneasily "HEPS was emanating an atypical soft high pitched sound. Staggering was to see TAK not only at the HEPS business end but also on top of the Proton Accumulator none-the-less, where I must have accidentally left it in my earlier haste to get to the Propulsion Research lab! Actually I was more than a little unnerved," I disclosed "because if the accelerator feeding the sequencer had overloaded, likely a dreadful explosion would occur thus destroying both the lab and TAKs instruments."

"I remember wondering," I acknowledged "whether my leaving TAK in such a potentially disastrous spot was the cause of the uncharacteristic sound. Without a pause to ponder," I continued "I charged into the shielded Control Room and commanded immediate HEPS shut-down! Intriguingly, the high pitched noise ceased when HEPS deactivated. I remember mumbling to the now quiescent HEPS, "Are these two events linked?""

"Without hesitating, I removed a Radiation Emissions Scanner (RES) from its cradle on the Control Room wall," I stated energetically "and immediately initiated a full spectrum analysis. As I slowly moved toward TAK, I carefully scrutinized the RES for any indication of harmful frequency variants. I was surprised the scan of the lab was nominal … without any indication of danger!"

"However, even though I detected no dangerous anomalies," I stated in an exasperated tone "I knew my HEPS research was going to be delayed because as you both know, safety protocols require suspension of all lab activities until the contamination folks pronounce 'all-clear'."

"Just as the safety crew arrived, a timer alert I had set on my AIM heads-up display indicated return to the Propulsion Research lab. Before heading out, I recall retrieving ART from its designated TAK pocket and slipping it into my pocket. As I was initiating the next phase of the Energy-Pulse Data (EPD) diagnostic cycle, I remember mentally noting that at least I'm on schedule in the Propulsion Research lab."

"I also remember suggesting to myself that 'perhaps the HEPS incident is a blessing' as its pause allows me time to work on my 'HoloSpheric Imager' passion project that I call HoloS. As I'm certain my HoloS research is also a key to my Away-event," I stated excitedly to Fyustre and Tsilerid "I believe crucial for your solutioning is 'bringing you up to speed' with my HoloS research! Is that OK with both of you?" I questioned. I was pleased both teammates were enthusiastic about continuing to listen!

"I conceived the now fully functional HoloS," I explained "as a means to render an encapsulating 4-dimensional real-time spherical hologram of the Kholesterian solar system. At the spheres elevated core awaits a gyroscopic chair, which is outfitted with not only a virtual command array but also a voice control interface to AIM. Once belted in, one can use either or both systems to rapidly present a real-time virtual view of every object within our solar system; and also from any desired observation point within the HoloS matrix."

"I can't wait to try HoloS out; it sounds fantastic," said an excited Tsilerid!

"The positive implications for safer travel within our solar system are exponential: fantastic job Divad," exclaimed Fyustre.

"Thank you both for your accolades ... they are priceless to me," I responded appreciatively! "My lead up story to the Away-event is nearly done. Again ... thank you for being so attentive!"

"So, once the next phase of the Energy-Pulse Data (EPD) diagnostic cycle was initialized," I continued "I headed to the HoloS lab. I was very excited to complete the remaining three prelaunch diagnostics, try out the gyroscopic chairs motion system and initialize HoloS's maiden 'voyage' preparations."

"When AIM verified diagnostics concluded without incident, I harnessed myself to the gyroscopic chair and instructed AIM to initiate HoloSs' pre go-live protocols. Immediately however, at about four arms lengths in front of me," I specified "HoloS was displaying a small redish pulsating blip. I could not think of any aspect in its design," I noted "that could cause a repeating blip; it was puzzling."

"My first notion was the holographic initiators as responsible for this blip event. However, as caution guided me to resolve the cause before continuing, I requested AIM probe for any comparable HoloS events. When AIM reported 'nothing similar', I concluded the blip was a harmless ghost fault."

"Sorry my backstory explanations are taking longer than expected," I stated apologetically "but I do not want to leave out something you two would find useful."

"No issue," responded Fyustre as Tsilerid nodded agreement "any detail could be the very clue we need!"

"Thanks to you both; your support is invaluable to me," I stated warmly.

"Pre-launch protocols," I continued "necessitate entering specific parameters and activating associated systems like the Launch Sequencer. However," I explained "to both accomplish the entries and initiate their sequences, necessary is for me to be within the HoloS envelope. Excited when all system indicators turned green, I exited HoloS, retrieved ART, which I put in my pocket, verified TAK contents (my Tech Analysis Kit items), and then hooked TAK onto my utility belt."

"Due to TAKs bulk however, ART felt uncomfortable in my pocket. So, I instead placed ART in a TAK compartment. Now ready for the next phase I stepped back inside HoloS, climbed into the gyroscopic chair and excitedly initiated the first live test."

"As you are both aware of the Away-event details," I validated and then added rhetorically "you ready to dive-in and figure-out the specifics that drove my incredible experience?"

Important to note for perspective that advanced as Kholesterians are in local planetary system terms, interstellar travel continues to be considered a most unlikely possibility. Although Kholesterians have almost half light-speed capable and comfortable vessels designed to commute within a few Blicktars (a Blicktar equals one billion miles), most believe venturing trillions and trillions of Blicktars into who knows what unpredictable fury is irrational.

Thus, keen and committed, we three, united with AIMs awesome capabilities began scrutinizing daunting accumulations of both scientific archives and media sources from the past two-hundred Cycles. Flagged were every potential nugget that might illuminate the connection of which we were certain must exist between Conduit theory and my Away-event.

Disheartening were the many occasions our diligence seemed to provide key solutioning nuggets, which upon deeper analysis concluded in dead ends. Clearly, even after our monumental efforts, we were unable to find any substantial archive data that would point us in a useful direction.

Hence, little did we foresee our 'Conduit' project would result in revealing technologies - gifted by an ancient race called the Kyorma'kren - that would facilitate almost instantaneous inter-galactic sojourns!

"After three Rotations of deep delving," Tsilerid stated bluntly "obvious the information we seek is non-existent. Thus, I suggest a different tactic. Instead of continuing what I am judging a fruitless search, let's instead reconstruct every detail of the day Vellyr experienced his two Away-events!"

"Brilliant idea Tsilerid," chimed Fyustre who added questioningly "is this detailed retracing approach okay with you Vellyr?"

"Definitely," I responded. "Prior to our collaboration I was working a similar strategy: trying to understand the causality of the Away-events.

"My expectation," Tsilerid shared eagerly "is that by recreating granular details of Vellyr's day and then re-enacting those pertinent in the correct sequence, probable we will be able to not only understand how to initiate an Away-event but also perhaps even unravel Conduit theory!"

"Wouldn't that be fantastic?" injected Fyustre! In other words, you are promoting that by the processes of logic and elimination we three will be able to recreate the Away-event through dissecting, digging-down and determining significant prior Away-event conditions."

ART

"**S**ounds like a solid plan to me," I validated. I'll fetch my work in progress list: back in a flash!" At that I headed to retrieve the list I had un-customarily written down in order to ensure no-one would discover it in AIM and conclude I was perpetrating a hoax. On my return I shared my activity list of the Away-event day.

Away-event days Chronology:
1. HEPS lab first thing THEN to
2. Propulsion Research lab (PRL): initiated Energy Pulse (EP) diagnostic
3. Realized I did not have TAK (my Tech Analysis Kit)
4. HEPS lab to retrieve TAK: high pitched sound on arrival
5. Saw TAK at the "Concentrator" business end of the Proton Accumulator (PA)
6. Shut HEPS down: sound stopped
7. Performed radiation check of lab and TAK
8. When nominal: I retrieved TAK
9. Safety team shut down HEPS
10. Retrieved TAK and put ART in my pocket

11. Back to PRL: initiated next phase; THEN to HoloS lab: ran pre-launch Diagnostics; sat in and checked Gyroscopic Chair (GC) functionality
12. Initiated HoloS maiden voyage prelims
13. Blip on HoloS display: AIM's analysis was nominal: all systems green
14. Exit HoloS to retrieve TAK
15. Re-enter HoloS; strapped into GC
16. Initiated first live test
17. Away-event one - 3 plus minutes: then back after touching a spot on the protective translucent shield with different shimmer
18. When back, I distanced myself from HoloS for about one-tenth of a Segment
19. Back into HoloS sphere: Initiate another test as before
20. Away-event two: 9 seconds then back; didn't touch shields differing spot this time
21. Initiate another same test: No Away-event
22. Initiated many more same tests: No Away-events
23. Thought I had gone crazy!

Tsilerid, Fyustre and I, attempting to determine the responsible anomaly (perhaps anomalies) scoured my list silently for quite a while. Fyustre was first to offer an observation, "The 'blip' was certainly not normal."

"Yes ... I agree," I confirmed "however, before launching the first HoloS test I did ask AIM to scrutinize archives for any other types of reported 'blips' in any journals in the last 150 Cycles. None were found!"

"I have noticed," Tsilerid submitted "two other potentially anomalous or not-normal occurrences from the list you provided: HEPS's high pitched sound and TAK placed at the collector end of HEPS."

"Thank you! Those are definitely on my list as well," I relayed. Additionally, I offer my most likely contenders: HEPS had never emitted any sound; HoloS had never presented a 'blip'; I had never initiated a live HoloS test; and I had never experienced an Away-event. Looking at this list leaves me a little disillusioned," I continued "as nothing dramatically jumps out as an obvious cause of my Away-events."

We each intently reread and pondered the list for some time trying to visualize the stream of events. "Here's my current summary of what I find pertinent," said Fyustre confidently "Vellyr entered and initiated HoloS; then the first longer 'space' experience; then Vellyr exited HoloS; then re-entered and re-initiated HoloS; then the second short 'space' experience; then subsequently initiated HoloS multiple times without a 'space' experience. Thing is," continued a frustrated Fyustre "I can neither peg what caused the difference between the first and second Away-event; nor the second Away-event and then none! What was different?"

"Your summaries have actually reminded me of an omission in my list of events. As I noted earlier, upon return from my first Away-event I distanced myself from HoloS. What I didn't remember 'til now is that when I got back into the gyro-chair (list item 19) to try again; nothing happened. Just then I realized I had left TAK behind, so I retrieved it before what turns out to be my third, not second attempt. That means the tool belt must be at least part of the answer!"

"Answer me this," Fyustre exclaimed "was ART in your TAK kit?"

"Definitely," I responded vaguely "when not in my hand, that's its home. Why?"

"My conclusion," Fyustre stated exuberantly "is more likely your 'space' experience has to do with ART than TAK; as all TAK kits are ostensibly identical … aren't they?"

"Yes … TAK's are mostly identical," I said with elevated enthusiasm. Mine is recognizable because its snap is unlike any other I have seen. Are you positing that something made ART work; and then something made ART not work?"

"Here's my extension of your proposal," stated an excited Tsilerid "as things need power to work, must be - if ART was key to the Away-events - that ART must somehow have been energized; and then somehow become discharged!"

"Before we assumption ourselves into a corner," Fyustre cautioned "let's first run a comparative analysis of other TAK's to confirm or debunk their similarity!"

At that stellar suggestion, I procured one new, and multiple unused TAK kits from their perches. On return, I removed the three automated devices and twelve manual tools from the new kit and laid them out on my left. I did the same for each of the three used kits; placing each of their kit contents in the same relative positions, but on my right. We carefully examined each item from both kit types in order to compare every aspect of each tool and carry case. All items from new and used kits checked-out as identical in every significant way. Although the used TAK kit's items and cases were more worn, we could discern no other variance.

"I believe we have proven," asserted Fyustre "ART not TAK should be the primary target of our investigations as it seems the most likely candidate!" Tsilerid and I agreed wholeheartedly.

"In other words," I stated quizzically "perhaps ART's power became perilously low during my second Away-event experience and therefore aborted the excursion?"

"Exactly … yes," chimed Fyustre "that would explain why the second Away-event was so short! You quit the first Away-event by touching what I assume is an area of the shield designed to allow the occupant to terminate their sojourn … just before ART's power was totally depleted. The second Away-event was short because that is all ART could sustain due to the tiny amount of energy remaining!"

"Big next questions then," I posited "how did ART either get powered or was it powered when found by my relative all those Cycles ago. Perhaps even a bigger question," I stated "is ART, which has always been considered created by a unique volcanic event, even of this planet!"

"You posed a boggling question my friend," said Tsilerid "perhaps determining its origins should wait until we can figure out if it became powered by something more recent?"

"While you were talking, I was inspired to recheck the list," said Fyustre "and the not-normal event of TAK being placed on top of the HEPS Proton Accumulator popped out because now we know ART was in TAK at the time!"

"And if that was the powering event," injected Tsilerid "we can easily verify or debunk the possibility ... right Divad?"

"If you are suggesting," I responded with angst "we put TAK atop the Collector Array of the Proton Accumulator again, be aware we would be crafting a literally explosive scenario! Not a good idea!"

"Actually," Fyustre clarified "I believe Tsilerid is suggesting putting only ART close to the Proton Concentrator for a short duration. Either ART's internal filaments brighten as you casually noted previously; or not."

"If they do," suggested Tsilerid "we can test ART to discover if the Away-event occurs again!"

As Tsilerid and Fyustre continued discussions, I removed ART from its TAK home, put it on the table between us and just contemplated ... for a long time. I was hoping the answers to both the "powered" and "origin" dilemmas might spontaneously reveal. I picked ART up, then felt and looked at every aspect of the so familiar object. ART just looked like ART should look. Revelations neither flashed into existence nor spontaneously appeared. I put ART back on the table.

I reflected back on ART's discovery in the ash of a volcano. Is it possible for a natural set of planetary events to both create ART in all its uniqueness and to provide the type of power that would make the Away-event possible? Although I had no data to back up my conclusion, every neuron of my dual brains was screaming: NO - not possible!

ART may have been formed in a star but certainly not on this planet. If ART was formed in a star or some other off planet - yet unknown - universe process, then fell burning through our thick dense atmosphere onto Kholesteria, explanation of some characteristics might be possible: smooth, pitted, oblong, clear.

The difficulty with that scenario became instantly evident. ART has been experimentally subjected to the most tumultuous processes existing on our world and has remained unaffected: totally impervious. I concluded it was unlikely a trip through our atmosphere would have any effect on ART's properties or physical attributes.

If I comply with my option that proposes ART originates from out in the universe somewhere, there are only two creation possibilities: natural or manufactured. Either option was boggling. On one hand, the chances of a naturally created item coincidentally interfacing with Kholesteria's technology thereby powering an Away-event had to be massively less than negligible.

On the other hand, the possibility of any other sentient race existing, let alone one so technologically advanced as to create such an item and then drop it off on Kholesteria or send it, or sending many of them (?), into the universe seemed likewise minute.

As there was no evident reconciling of my two options, I decided to reread my list of known occurrences. Operating theories: ART had power since it was located, then lost or used it; or ART became powered, then lost or used it.

My strong tendency was toward the "became powered" second option, mostly from recollecting that ART's nine filaments seemed slightly brighter before my first Away-event than I had ever noticed. The second option gave some hope of reconstructing the Away-event while the first did not limit itself to current events; thus creating many indeterminate variables.

If ART "became powered" the question, "was ART recently exposed to any unique circumstances", required an answer which would satisfy the second "became powered" proposition.

Thinking back to when I had taken ART from its sanctuary inside TAK, I remembered I had an uneasy feeling: fringe awareness that something familiar was now different. I dismissed the vague impression because my prevailing focus was to quickly return to HoloS.

What was different? What was different? It wasn't just the squeal or my personal discontent about placing TAK in a potentially explosive place; there was something else! What had created my sensation of uneasiness? I closed my eyes and calmed myself; hoping to recall the moment. I visualized removing TAK from its dangerous "Concentrator" position; putting TAK on an adjoining bench; reaching into TAK for ... ART!

My eyes popped open! Excitement surged through me! The rush was more powerful than performing my first spiral jump off our planets highest cliff. I am now sure: The coloured filaments inside ART ... some were different!

Instead of being almost imperceptible a few were brighter or thicker or somehow more obvious! I knew ART extremely well having manipulated it in one hand or the other for many, many Cycles. I was right! The difference was just barely perceptible when I retrieved ART: that fringe awareness was the cause of my uneasy feeling ... for sure!

The next realization struck me like I imagine it would feel to be struck by an electrical discharge in a severe tempest. The minor changes in a few of ART's coloured filaments must be due to HEPS. TAK was placed dangerously close to the Proton Concentrator end of HEPS. Some small amount of the masses of Proton energy bombarding the Concentrator must have transferred into ART. Nothing, even partially similar had ever been recorded in the history of our people.

I involuntarily sat down feeling too flimsy to stand. My mind, without a comparative base of similar events, was struggling to resolve the incomprehensibility of the situation. It was attempting to cope with the repercussions of accidentally uncovering a fantastic new reality.

"Excuse me for interrupting your thinking process," I stated apologetically "but while you were in discourse I replayed the events of the day in question and am confident the Away-events may very well be a repeatable enactment of the Conduit theory."

Moments later I smiled and chuckled to myself for the first time since I had been awe struck by the realization we were on the threshold of uncovering how to deploy a totally new, society changing technology.

"Obviously," I smiled broadly again "the best irrefutable evidence is to provide the Away-event experience to sceptics! ART is the key to providing such a demonstration: more specifically, the capability I firmly believe ART brought to the equation."

"Thus," I re-confirmed "I agree with you both we should initiate investigation by reconstructing the conditions, which powered ART. Everything hinges on our being able to make that happen!"

At this we dived in: all three totally convinced we would succeed. "There are several 'knowns' in the equation," I detailed "that I am positive will allow us to create Away-events. For instance, HEPS output level - retrievable from the data-stream logs; TAK's proximity to the Concentrator - definitely reproducible; ART was inside TAK - easy to duplicate. With any luck ART would power if I put TAK back in a similar position."

Even while my gut told me our task was not going to be easy, I remained steadfastly optimistic. I retrieved the HEPS logs. Upon scrutiny, we realized there was negligible Proton stream variance recorded from HEPS initiation through my terminating the process after hearing the squeal. Using the logs as a guide we set the parameters to emulate last evening's settings.

As an additional precaution we performed a series of broadband electromagnetic readings: They were nominal. I instructed AIM to perform similar readings throughout the coming experimental trials and give an audible alert if any readings strayed out of our specified range. We would engage HEPS once the other experimental conditions were in place.

I reclaimed ART from its current resting place on the table and sidled over to TAK positioned a little further along on the bench. I opened TAK and placed ART in its usual upper pocket.

I had some trepidation placing TAK back at the Concentrator's danger spot. Even though we trusted both the instilled parameters and AIM's capability to monitor and alert for any hazardous conditions, this placement was not without risk. Additionally, we had no idea how to find out if anything significant was actually occurring to ART.

"We will need to be very cautious," suggested Tsilerid "that we are not interrupted."

"Not to worry," I responded "HEPS and HoloS labs are designated for my exclusive use; thus, minimal chance of being disturbed. To perform the HoloS side of the Away-event reconstruction though, it will be necessary to wait until the outer area is vacated."

At that confirmation we three headed into the HEPS lab where I took up position at the Concentrator end of HEPS.

Before proceeding we reviewed our first attempts procedural order: Position TAK - relying on my best-guess memory; engage AIM from within the protected control room - after establishing the alert and monitor parameters; bring HEPS on-line; monitor HEPS until auto-shutdown - I set this to the approximate duration ART was exposed on Away-event night; if HEPS started squealing again, hit the emergency override.

A quick double check of critical parameters and I brought HEPS on line. HEPS does not generate sound, thus the lab is normally whisper quiet. Tonight was no exception.

As I initiated the process I felt electrified with expectation. We were really eager to hear HEPS squeal. We attentively evaluated the many displays while actively interacting with the labs AIM pod. I was determined to be prepared for any indication or sign of pending disaster.

Marking the way to our first attempts ultimate conclusion AIM's duration display advanced relentlessly: 10%, 30%, 50% of the determined elapsed time. All was stable: no readings or noises out of the ordinary.

Indicators were nominal; we could have been monitoring a lump of billion Cycle old lava. We continued observing: 70%; 90%; 100%. I verified to ensure the HEPS automatic shutdown had engaged at the precise programmed termination time limit: it had.

I must admit my excitement level was slightly diminished when this attempt did not result in the squeal, which I had idealistically considered the success indicator.

Regardless, we were determined to move forward as rapidly as possible. Resolutely we continued with the next validation and verification steps: retrieve ART from TAK; kick up HoloS; establish its parameters; test to see if an Away-event occurs.

After removing ART from TAK, we each looked long and hard at its filaments. We were not sure if any of the filaments were brighter: maybe a little more visible? Obviously, we were no longer unbiased observers as we were completely corrupted by intense desire to have this experiment conclude successfully. Time for speculation was past: it was now try HoloS time!

Our hopes were high as I happily hummed my way to the HoloS lab!

With all HoloS and ancillary systems operating as per AIM's log of the first Away-event, I moved toward HoloS, mouths bone dry with nervousness. We had placed ART in precisely the same compartment in the exact same TAK diagnostic kit. One final check: all was as it should be. I slipped into the gyroscopic chair;

initiated protocols as I had the first time; and …
Nothing?!

We regrouped quickly by assessing if anything, even the
smallest item or protocol, had been omitted. There was
no oversight: even my garments were the same!

Back to the drawing board! Well maybe that analysis was
a little rash. After all, the basis of our premise is that
ART needs power. Even though unsure ART's filaments
were glowing ever so slightly moments ago, it was now
evident that they were not.

Before I entered HoloS, we had thought to render a
highest-capture holographic image of ART. After taking
an after image, we displayed both images on the three
dimensional holographic display. We used our own
senses and the full array of AIM sensors to assess any
variance: There was none. ART was the same on the way
in as now. The only conclusion possible: ART had not
been powered, or powered insufficiently, in the HEPS
lab. We headed back to see if AIM could provide some
HEPS clues.

At my request AIM reanalyzed the HEPS data packets
from the recent "charging" process. No insights were
presented.

Proceeding with our theory of ART providing the Away-
event power, still seemed the superior assumption. We
decided to prolong ART's HEPS exposure: However,
with four enhancements.

First: As ART is the focus, TAK will be discarded from the equation. With ART liberated from TAK, we will be able to visually monitor changes in ART's filaments.

Second: We fashioned a cradle in which ART can be manipulated into different positions. One major supposition invests in the possibility that ART's position within TAK was critical to ART's power accumulation. In other words, the foundation of my first attempt was built on remembering and re-enacting TAK's and therefore ART's positions relative to the HEPS Concentrator. Thus, ART's position was likely incorrect.

Third: We devised a Positioning Grid in order to bracket the selected parameters: the criterion is my best-guess memory regarding ART's position - as similar to the recent attempt as I can muster. I thought to myself, "This process would be so much more refined if I had thought to initiate AIM to record ART's original TAK position."

Regardless, our starting point assumes ART would have been resting diagonally with its long side about forty-five degrees, to the HEPS Proton stream. The rotational series plan requires 360 linear repositions of ART in one degree increments; perpendicular to HEPS directional flow. AIM will be engaged to verify positioning accuracy, to record the event stream and to detect and notify of any change in ART's brightness.

Fourth: Initiate the first trials with shorter HEPS exposure beginning with ten percent of the original events duration. If additional trials are necessary increment time duration by ten percent increases.

Looking at possible combinations and duration of each trial we realized this process could take significant time! Considering the expected outcome though, we were very anxious to begin as only 6 Segments remained before the start of the Innovation Festival and our presentation!

"Okay," said Fyustre excitedly "as you introduced us to this Away-event project, Tsilerid and I would like you to be the one to place ART for its first iteration!"

"Thank you for the honor," I bowed appreciatively while smiling broadly with appreciation. Here goes. ART is verified by Tsilerid and I to be in position one. Fyustre," I requested "would you instruct AIM to run the first HEPS segment please!"

"Happy to," responded Fyustre. At that AIM displayed a countdown of the prearranged one Khol short duration.

When the countdown completed without any squealing I asked, "AIM, did you register any changes in ART?"

"Yes," said AIM "a nearly imperceptible 0.003 uptick of ART's refraction index, which could have been caused by variances in the labs ambient light."

"As no squeal occurred," I stated confidently "let's continue our testing by doubling the duration as planned." As no objections were offered, Fyustre initialized the test just after AIM displayed the prearranged two Khol countdown.
"Apparently doubling the exposure time did not cause a squeal either," I stated happily! Did you register any changes AIM?"

"Yes," said AIM: "A refraction index increment of plus 1.116, which unambiguously originates from ART."

When we looked at ART, and its filaments were noticeably brighter, I don't think any of us has ever been so excited. "I am sure this result means ART is capturing HEPS Proton energy," Tsilerid stated with unbridled exuberance: Let's triple the original timeframe to validate!"

"Fyustre, please instruct AIM to run the third scenario," I said with bubbling over expectation.

"I am so nervous and excited," Fyustre shared as she primed the next test and watched AIM's countdown from three Khols.

When AIM's countdown reached zero, "Still no squeal from HEPS even after tripling the exposure time," I stated with happy surprise. "AIM, did you register any changes this time?"

"Yes," said AIM: "A refraction index increment of plus 3.759. This indicates ART's power accumulation is exponential, not linear."

"I vote we take ART over to the HoloS lab right now," stated Tsilerid decisively "and discover if an Away-event occurs!"

"I think that a grand idea," Fyustre and I chimed almost simultaneously to which I added "which of you would like to trial the first collaborative Away-event?"

Tsilerid immediately responded, "I insist Fyustre have the honor of Cre'ators first sojourn," to which Fyustre replied while emphatically palming all four hands toward Tsilerid "no ... I insist you be first!"

"Relax ladies," I injected "the single gyroscopic chair I have been using is interchangeable with one that comfortably accommodates two ... so both of you are going!"

"You are a rascal," both said almost simultaneously while presenting huge smiles!

"I would recommend," stated AIM "one more three Khol millisegment charge cycle should first be performed so we can closely calculate the duration of a full charge."

When the fourth charge cycle was completed, Sting announced, "I registered a refraction index increment of plus 9.759, which means a full charge from zero would require approximately 2500 Kyters or 50 Khols or one Segment or 1/20 of the planets Rotation."

"Thanks Sting," I said thankfully "with the current charge what do you calculate will be their maximum duration?"

"Insufficient data is available. Thus," Sting responded "I recommend a limit of 5.0 minutes. On return, I will check ART's refraction index to assess the Away-events power consumption."

"Thanks once again AIM," we three appreciatively responded simultaneously!

Both Tsilerid and Fyustre were strapped into the swapped out dual Gyro-chair the briefest flash after the Robo-mechs had locked it in place.

I wasted no time initializing HoloS. They simply disappeared!

At the finish of AIM's 5 minute countdown they both reappeared as if they had never left. "I believe we just orbited the planet you described in your first Away-event," blurted Tsilerid.

"Unbelievably fantastic," bubbled Fyustre as they dismounted from the gyro-chair.

Just then AIM displayed the following message on its Holographic display:

"I am Sting, a friendly sentient artificial intelligence assisting the sentient race called Humans in a distant Galaxy called 'The Milky Way' on a planet called Earth into whose proximity I brought your two Kholesterian adventurers. Ambassadors will visit soon and openly share knowledge and technology. This will include locating your planets 'Sting', which will enable you to control the Kyorma'kren technology you call ART."

Appendix

Dyonne-01

Thus, to ensure we are all equally informed regarding Universe-H's driving forces, I'll take an extended moment to expand and expose its pertinent clandestine workings."

"In other words," Dyonne continued thoughtfully "to clearly understand one's VibrationSignature, first necessary is to both comprehend Universe-H's energy foundations or baseplate; and second, how it's stringent rules enable creation of ever more complex Matter 'stuff'. Exposure of Universe-H's baseplate," Dyonne explained "is necessary because, as we are contained within Universe-H boundaries, we must by default abide by its operating parameters or Laws: No choice there!"

"So, down to the core of Universe-H's functionality we go," Dyonne said playfully. At the very core of Universe-H conjectured are twelve (12) BaseOne energySignatures. Abbreviated BOES, they are the 'baseEnergy building-blocks' for ever more complex Mass constructs. Think of it this way," suggested Dyonne excitedly "BOES combinations are the literal building-blocks for all more complex Universe-H constructs: Bosons, Quarks, Neutrons, Protons, Electrons, Atoms, Molecules, Compounds and so forth, up the Mass 'size' scale."

"Fantastically, BaseOne linkages are the underpinnings that enable creation of not only all non-corporeal (or not-alive) physical 'Matter' wonders from atoms like iron, to compounds like sugar, and larger inorganic physical 'stuff' like mountains, but also corporeal (or living) organisms like Mankind. Consequently, as one climbs the rungs from BaseOne to BaseEight formulation as a Human biological entity, lots of more complex linkages have occurred: Molecules (BaseFour), Compounds (BaseFive), Cells (BaseSix) and Tissues (BaseSeven)."

"Conclusively, whether the 12 BaseOne frequency underpinnings assemble into corporeal Matter complexities or endure to provide the vast Mass repositories of non-corporeal 'soup' enabling animation, BaseOne frequencies and their selective bonding interplays are not only the basis for all that exists in Universe-H but also what ensures Universe-H's sustainability."

"In other words, the 12 BaseOne frequencies and their selective linkage combinations are the essential foundations which underlie all more complex Universe-H constructs; and expansively, both its continuation and our existence."

"To review then," Dyonne stated joyously "the EFS is significant because it provides an extremely precise and useful register upon which can be slotted the not only known and theorized frequencies but also their juxtapositions. Simply stated, the EFS provisions an immutable frequency 'spot' on its very long gradient or linear-scale for all the energy and matter stuff in Universe-H."

"In other words," Dyonne continued to summarize "the Electromagnetic Frequency Spectrum cataloguing extends from the smallest known energy remnant to the many atomic level matter expressions (like Hydrogen and

Oxygen); to molecular compounds formed of precursor atomic building-block 'material' (like water); to vast arrays of cooperatively interacting molecular compounds (like DNA, which spawns Life-Forms and their many diverse Species); right up to Universe-H itself."

"Synchronously, as Mankind harmonicallyVibrates within a narrow frequencyRange, Mankind also has its position on the Electromagnetic Frequency Spectrum. Thus, explanation of Divad's gift must be contiguous with Universe-H's frequencyBaseplate or baseEnergy components. Let's disclose the scientific facts that are primary to understanding the roots of one's particular VibrationSignature.

"Repeat alert," Dyonne chuckled "one's VibrationSignature spawns from two sources. Our BIOVibe 'Dive' is first then. To decode what spawns one's BIOVibe and one's EXVibe, understanding of Universe-H's grassroots must be clear. As you all know, and I only reiterate for continuity, fundamental is that throughout Universe-H each and every Matter and Energy bit vibrate at their very specific frequency. Not surprisingly then, as we are 100% made of Universe-H stuff, our physical selves as well as our experiences (which remember are actionPotential energy storehoused as archivedOld) also vibrate."

"The first part to explain Divad's 'recognition' by The-Walls must therefore focus on aspects that uniquely vibrate your physical-self (one's body or biology): i.e., what causes your physical-self's harmonicVibration or BIOVibe. For instance, not only do life sustaining elements in our body, like iron, potassium, sodium, calcium, etc. all vibrate differently, but also do the myriads of complex compounds that comprise our physical selves uniquely vibrate: like water, arrays of enzymes, hormones, and so forth."

"Similar to individual instruments in a symphony orchestra that form magnificent harmonic sounds, so are beautiful distinctive harmonicFrequencies produced by the unique bonding interplay of physical-self's vast array of elemental components. Stated differently, one's BIOVibe is formed from all the myriads of variant harmonic resonances produced by one's physical-self elements.

"Next 'Dive' examines how one's EXVibe is actualized. "Provable is that one's distinctive experience accumulations as archivedOld (which recall is frequencyEnergy or actionPotential) also holistically (i.e., all accumulated actionPotential) vibrate. Unique holistic vibration, which is scientifically measurable, is due to vast multitudes of actionPotential frequencies (i.e., electrical-energy equivalents of sensoryAccepted mechanical-energy 'Clues' as to WhatIsGoingOnOutThere) being retained as archivedOld in extensive arrays of DataArchives."

"Stated differently, the second part of the explanation thus focuses on the role archivedOld, which is storehoused in neural realEstate, plays in manifesting one's VibrationSignature. Clearly, as the diverse repositories of archivedOld (established in myriads of frequency specific DataArchives) harmonicallyVibrate: so too does one's cerebral neural realEstate holistically vibrate. Thus, as a consequence of unique experiences, or stated differently a person's unique sensoryAcceptance combinations, each person's neural realEstate produces a different harmonicVibration, which is termed EXVibe."

"In other words, because experiences are retained as variously vibrating actionPotential frequencies in archivedOld cerebral neural realEstate or dataArchives, and as experience mix varies person-to-person due to variances in sensoryAcceptance; the DataArchive blends of actionPotential consequently vary between people."

"Stated differently, DataArchives do not vibrate generically person-to-person, but instead present a unique holistic frequency (harmonicVibration) in each person. Thus, one's actionPotential accumulations, which are storehoused in multiple DataArchives as archivedOld, yield a unique holistic harmonicVibration or EXVibe."

"Excitingly, due to harmonicBlending of one's BIOVibe and EXVibe, everyone presents a unique holistic VibrationSignature. Variance of EXVibe is also true of twins, triplets, quadruplets, etc. Although their BIOVibe may be ostensibly identical, their EXVibes can be radically different due to the archivedOld retention of divergent experiences. Thus, as each emanates a unique VibrationSignature, so too do they exhibit unique personalities and behaviors.

"Know that whereas genetics dictates both BioMatter extents and brainMass capacity; experiences provide the fill, content or archivedOld that manifests one's EXVibe."

"Fantastically one's VibrationSignature is not fixed! Instead it continuously revises throughout one's lifetime due to both physical changes and experience acquisition. Thus, one's baby-self harmonically vibrated differently than one's adolescent-self, than one's current grown-self, than will one's future-self."

"Perhaps the reason most love Babies is due to the fact that a newborn's neural realEstate contains minimal cerebral actionPotential (and thus EXVibe). In other words, at birth a baby's VibrationSignature is almost pure genetically rendered BIOVibe."

... To be continued ...